Tony Rao lives in Kent, England with two children studying at university. This book is the culmination of twenty years of listening to the narratives of people living in an area founded on the docks and the drinking culture within it. He came to write his first book to put his experiences into words for a topic that is close to his heart. His professional work has involved improving opportunities for marginalized groups over the years. Experience in having a family member with a severe and enduring mental illness has also been used within the novel to enhance the storyline.

Tony Rao

Catch Me When I Fall

Austin Macauley Publishers™
London • Cambridge • New York • Sharjah

A CIP catalogue record for this title is available from the British Library.

ISBN 9781398406476 (Paperback)
ISBN 9781398406483 (ePub e-book)

www.austinmacauley.com

First Published (2021)
Austin Macauley Publishers Ltd
25 Canada Square
Canary Wharf
London
E14 5LQ

I could not have written this without you, my wife. Your time, patience and constant support kept me going. As you read each chapter, you laughed and cried with me. I got there in the end!

My lovely children were always there to provide a welcome distraction at times when it seemed that no progress was being made.

The community mental health team where I have been for 22 years has changed constantly but my own nurses have stuck by me and shared with me and joys and sorrows of caring for a population of older people who have not asked for much but have needed a lot. Especially John, who have read through draft after draft and eased its passage to the final product.

My fellow psychiatrists have stopped at nothing to offer their encouragement. But above all, it is my patients who have made this book possible by letting me into their encouragement and by letting me into their lives to share their tales. Tales that will live long in my memory of my beloved.

To the people of Bermondsey,

past, present and future.

Chapter 1

Patient P, Bed 3

It was the first time that Peggy had felt this woozy after a drink, as she sat back in Jim's chair, peering through her net curtains at the pigeons pecking at her windowsill. She hadn't thought twice before pouring a second one, but this time she'd been drinking on an empty stomach. Mixed with medication for blood pressure, it may all have been too much for her system. As she got up to go to the toilet, she felt the television picture becoming gradually more blurred and toppled over, crashing to the ground. She had tried to hold onto the table to break her fall, but it only made things worse, as she caught her shoulder on the radiator. In the process, the table turned on its side, its erstwhile contents; a packet of peppermint creams, firing across the room like bullets from a Tommy gun; closely followed by pair of bifocals and a recently opened box of tissues. As she lay there, she found that she couldn't move. *Is this what happens when you have a stroke?* She knew that it made you wobbly and then incapacitated. How she wished that she had listened to Pat and Babs. They'd always insisted she wear a panic alarm for emergencies just like this. Peggy had fallen once before when her right knee gave way the week after Jim died. No bones broken – or at least that's what she hoped. She hadn't wanted to trouble the doctor over something so minor.

She attempted to sit up but felt too weak, so she called out, hoping that her next-door neighbour might hear her.

It was late, so maybe a lost cause.

"Help me! Rene. Can you hear me, Rene?"

There was a deathly hush from next door. After a few more desperate and louder pleas, she heard voices in conversation, then a series of loud raps on the door.

"Peggy! Is that you, luv? Are you OK?"

"Rene. I've had a fall. Can you get help for me, please?"

Rene had a key, as many neighbours do, so it didn't take long for the lock to turn and Rene to make an entrance, together with her husband, Michael.

"Michael, go and call the ambulance, luv."

The receiver back on the hook, Michael joined Rene, who had already tried unsuccessfully to help Peggy up. Peggy lay in a helpless crumpled heap on the living room carpet.

"I'm just doing the side-stroke, Rene." Peggy couldn't resist a small quip, even in her darkest moments.

"Oh, Peggy, how can you lark around at a time like this? You might have broken something, luv."

"I hope not; I was just getting into that crime drama on the telly."

Peggy didn't appear to be in any immediate danger, but Rene wasn't taking any chances and the ambulance was on its way.

The distant *wheow wheow wheow* of the ambulance siren grew progressively louder as it weaved its way through the estate and terminated abruptly.

The net curtains twitched as Rene cast a furtive glance thirteen floors down. A closer inspection revealed two uniformed figures, a man and a woman, in traditional green attire, opening the back of the ambulance and hauling out a stretcher. The lift had been particularly temperamental over Christmas and Peggy had found herself having to walk up and down all twelve flights of stairs on two occasions. But this time, she was in luck and the ambulance people thankfully didn't need to have a cardiac workout, particularly at this late hour on a deep, crisp and even winter's evening.

"Mrs Lighterman, we've just come to check you out."

They could see that Peggy was breathing normally, speaking clearly and fluently and there was no loss of blood and no sign of head injury.

"Can you move your arms and legs?" Peggy wiggled her hand and feet.

"I can't do the Hokey Cokey, but I can say Ra Ra Ra!" Peggy bellowed triumphantly.

"That's just as well, Mrs Lighterman."

The ambulance crew had seen it all. Aggressive young men on a night out. Road traffic accidents. Even buoyant older women with a sense of humour that could transcend even the most serious of maladies. Detecting no head or neck injury and no spinal damage, one of them went down to fetch up a wheelchair.

"I'll come along peacefully, officer," joked Peggy. The alcohol was beginning to wear off but had undoubtedly added to this rather bizarre sense of mirth that Peggy had mustered, given the situation in which she found herself. After helping her up into the wheelchair, it was time to go.

"Are we going to 999 Letsby Avenue?"

With that, she fell promptly asleep in the wheelchair, until finally waking up in a hospital bed.

Peggy had a less than vivid memory of what had happened. She had fallen at home. Hearing her cries for help, someone must have called an ambulance. The rest was a haze. Although in A&E for some hours, she couldn't for the life of her remember anything about it. Her head now a little clearer, she knew that she was on Patience Ward at St Saviour's Hospital. If Jim could only see her now. What had she come to? She was falling apart at the seams. A proper invalid it would seem. She took a deep breath in and exhaled with a half yawn, half sigh.

The clock was placed so high up on the wall, she had to stretch her neck to see it. It was 4pm. A voice rang out from behind the nursing station.

"Peggy. Peggy, 'ow are you, dear? I came as quick as I could, luv. When I got no answer from the bell, I let meself in. I was worried sick 'til I asked Rene from next door. She was the one that called the ambulance when she heard you calling out. Took 'em ages I 'urd, you being on the top floor and all that.

"You woz right as rain when I saw you yesterday. Looks like you 'ad a real nasty tumble. I 'ope you ain't broken nothing."

Pat moved towards the bed, her posture slightly stooped. The wear and tear on her spine from years of bending over a biscuit factory conveyor belt had taken its toll. She lay the grapes down on the side table, wedging them in the only space that she could find, between an empty green hospital cup and a copy of the South London Press.

"'Ere. I got you something."

She pushed her eyes towards the fruit, wrapped lovingly in a non-descript brown paper bag. Peggy propped herself up in her bed. At first, sliding back down the smooth surface of the rubber hospital mattress. She pushed herself higher, this time adjusting her back to get into a more comfortable position.

"Thank you, Pat. I really don't know what I would do without you."

Her voice was crisp, every syllable clearly enunciated. The product of a grammar school education. She had been the lucky one. A Levels, teacher training, college and a career that had made her feel valued. She'd been given wings but had kept her roots. Still living just around the corner from where she was born. Still as close to Pat and Babs as she had ever been. Of course, once there was Jim. How could she have survived without Jim? Her rock.

Always there through thick and thin. Never a bad word. Never a raised voice. The man of her dreams. Her teenage sweetheart. But she couldn't bear to think of what he would say if he could see her now. He was gone, and nothing was going to bring him back. Pat said her goodbye and left, but not before planting a hurried kiss on Peggy's left cheek.

"Nurse! Help me, nurse. Please, help me. Please. Oh. Oh. Where are you, nurse?"

She looked 'round to her right. A large plethoric man attached to a drip was holding on to the side of his bed, coughing, spluttering and clearly out of breath. A nurse finally arrived.

"Bill. You'll have a nasty fall if you try and get up on your own." Her voice left a sweet echo that lapped the detergent soaked hospital air.

The visitors started to trickle away until all she could hear was the whirr of a blood pressure machine, slowly inflating and deflating at regular intervals. Supper was offered, but she wasn't hungry. Four small dry sandwiches, a banana, fruit yoghurt and orange juice just didn't seem that appetising. Maybe if she was back in the Girl Guides. But this wasn't supper as she knew it. While reading a copy of the Southwark Gazette, another hour had ticked by. Just then, a figure emerged from the corridor. With a stethoscope draped around his neck and a six-o'clock shadow that looked more like ten o'clock, a doctor appeared.

"Mrs…"

He looked at his notes.

"Mrs Lighterman. Hello, my name is Dr Slater."

He glanced down again at his notes, looked back up and smiled. The sort of weary smile that doctors have when coming to the end of their shift.

"I've been a bit delayed on one of the other wards. Sorry about that. I hope you don't mind me asking you a few things about how you have been and then have a quick look at you?"

"No, Doctor. That's perfectly fine. Just don't ask me to repeat 'Peter Piper Picked a Peck of Pickled Peppers' ten times while standing on my head."

"Not this time," came the reply, as Dr Slater adjusted his notes, his eyes lighting up as he let out a muffled laugh.

"So, Mrs Lighterman…"

"Peggy is fine. Call me Peggy."

"So, Peggy. What brought you into hospital?"

"An ambulance, I think."

There was an awkward silence.

"Sorry, I couldn't resist that. I'll be a good patient now, Doctor. Please do continue."

The questions seemed to last an eternity, but the doctor was polite and professional throughout the clinical encounter. When he had finished his examination, he left just as quickly as he had arrived. Another ward. Another patient. Another hour before the end of his working day. Peggy reflected on what had just happened.

He hadn't asked her about her drinking. What would he have thought of her if she'd told him the truth? Would he think that she was an alcoholic? Would he have moved her to the nuthouse? Anyway, it really didn't matter. It's not as if she had a drinking problem. She had felt a bit woozy after her second glass of gin, but that was just her age. People fall all the time and that was the end of it. She sank back into her bed, pulled the sheets up to her chin and gradually fell into a slumber, the like of which she had not experienced since the funeral. *Strange that,* she thought, before finally closing her eyes and bidding the world goodnight. The deep sleep transported her back. Right back.

As she sat up in bed in a cold, damp room in Nickleby Square, she could hear her mother and mother's friends singing downstairs…

"We know our manners
Spend all our tanners
We are respected wherever we go
When you're roamin' down the Ol' Kent Road
All the win ders open wide

I tiddly I ti I ti I
I tiddly I ti I ti I
We are the Bermondsey Girls."

A light shone in her eyes. She awoke with a start.

"Sorry, Peggy, just checking if everything is all right."

The night nurse whispered something to her colleague as they carried out their evening nursing round. It was 11pm. The shiny metal framed tube light covering the ceiling of Bay 1 was so bright, it was as if she were staring into the sun. She drifted back to sleep again, back into the sultry summer haze of an oneirophrenic mirage.

"Peg. Peg, luv. It's gettin' late. We've gotta go 'ome now."

Her eyelids flickered, slowly opening one eye, peering around her momentarily and closing it quickly again.

"Come on, Peg. You go' school tomorrow and I'm not waitin' around while I've got work to do. And put something 'round you, luv. You'll catch your death of cold like that."

The beach at St Leonard's on sea was empty, save herself and Mum. Dad, Pat and Babs had started walking towards the car, their figures silhouetted against the shiny white background of Marine Court. Slowly, she rose, slipping back into the sand for a moment, but then summoning all her strength to push herself up again. Sand covered her back like a beige patchwork quilt clinging on to her skin, its glistening grains like dancing fireflies in the last remnants squeezed out from the late evening sun.

"Get off me! Stop it. What are you doing? Get off!"

"Jimmy. We need to change you."

Jimmy was having none of it. Amidst the background hum of the visiting time chatter, there was clearly something afoot behind the curtain of Bay 1, Bed 5.

After much ado, Jimmy had calmed down and some form of semblance had returned. One of the nurses pulled the curtain back around its track and all was well with the world. Peggy shut her eyes again, hoping for one last attempt at a decent sleep.

"Cummon, Peg, let's play Muffin Man!" Pat led her by the hand out of the house. Babs soon followed. She was Barbara really, but everyone called her Babs. The 'terrible three' their mother called them. Always looking out for each other and only apart during school time. They joined a larger group of children at the street corner.

There were at least twenty girls in all (she hadn't counted exactly but was usually quite good at estimating numbers). All stood in a large circle, with one of them outside…

"Oh, have you seen the muffin man, the muffin man, the muffin man. Oh, have you seen the muffin man that lives in Drury Lane? Oh…"

The girl danced around the ring as they sang. After a further two lines of the song, a second would be chosen. So, the song went on until all girls had been chosen and there was no one left to sing. She remembered many more of those singing games. Dusty Bluebells, with children weaving in and out of arches created by other holding hands and raising them above their heads. Then there was Lucy Locket, sung to the tune of Yankee Doodle Dandy.

She had slept barely a couple of hours. It was two in the morning. Outside was pitch black, with the only light coming from the streets and houses in the distance, like tiny beads spat out by the sun, slowly melting in a volcano of emptiness. Sleeping in fits and starts, she tossed and turned. Bill and Jimmy had, between them, created such a veritable cacophony, even Rip Van Winkle would have had insomnia. The bed was hard, and the pillows did not provide the snug comfort to which she had become accustomed in her own home. Awake again, she squinted at the clock above the entrance to her bay. It was seven in the morning. How she looked forward to being back in her own bed. She hoped it wouldn't be long before she'd be given the all-clear.

The morning performance had started between Jimmy and George, with several others joining in. It was time for morning medicine and then breakfast. Barely had she finished her last spoonful of porridge, when a large group of people approached her bed. There must have been ten of them, at least. The man at the front looked older than the rest. Short in stature, with receding grey hair, metal-rimmed glasses and benign demeanour. Standing next to him, she recognised Dr Slater from the night before, as well as the nurse who had taken her blood pressure and made her comfortable when she came onto the ward. The older man started speaking.

"Mrs Lighterman?"

"I hope so," came the reply. "But don't tell anyone or they'll all want that name."

The entourage broke into fits of laughter. After raising a mild smile, he continued.

"Mrs Lighterman. My name is Dr Dixon and I am your consultant."

He turned to Dr Slater in expectation of a briefing.

"So. This is Mrs Peggy Lighterman, a 70-year-old widow…"

"69, Doctor. I'm 69. It's 10 January 2003 and I was born on 7 March 1933. It's not March yet, Doctor." Peggy wondered how simple mental arithmetic could be so difficult for someone with so much education. The three Rs were obviously now the two Rs!

Dr Slater turned a shade of red that Peggy had only seen at the traffic lights when crossing the Old Kent Road. His voice faltered. He cleared his throat and took out a tissue to blow his nose, nearly dropping his mini-TV screen in the process.

"…a 69-year-old widow who presented with a mechanical fall at home."

Dr Dixon looked re-assured by Dr Slater's ability to regain his composure, notwithstanding his mathematical ineptitude.

"She has a history of hypertension, GERD, CKD stage 1 and OA. There is a family history of alcoholic liver disease in her father…"

Peggy felt a shiver running down her spine. She so hoped that the consultant had not heard this.

"…Mrs Lighterman lives alone in a 13th floor council flat on the Chuzzlewit Estate. Her husband had oat cell carcinoma and died in September last year.

"Mrs Lighterman is independent with all daily activities and has social support from her two sisters. Systems review was normal and on examination, there were no abnormalities…"

"Blood investigations?" Dr Dixon seemed keen to move on.

"MCV was mildly raised…" Dr Slater continued. Peggy switched off at that point.

Most of what she had heard was gobbledygook. Dr Dixon pointed to one of the younger contingents of the group.

"What are common causes of falls in older people?" The student looked blank, while the other put up her hand.

"Yes?"

"Postural instability?" she retorted, somewhat unsure of her answer.

"Good. I am sure that Dr Slater can go through the differential diagnosis with you later. Right…"

Dr Dixon leaned over slightly to make better eye contact with Peggy.

"I'm pleased to say that you can go home today, Mrs Lighterman."

Peggy heaved a sigh of relief but for more than one reason. He hadn't asked her about her drinking, though hidden in plain sight. Even she knew that alcohol damages your liver. But then again, who would ever think asking a retired teacher if she drinks. Not even a doctor, it would seem. For Peggy, this was a temporary reprieve. The procession moved on like a flock of sheep in order of seniority, with Dr Slater scuttling behind to catch up, furtively checking his TV screen as he did. Still further behind were the two medical students. One looked back at her and smiled politely before turning back 'round to join what was now a more elongated flotilla. Before she knew it, the hospital car had arrived. She didn't need a wheelchair, but the porter said that it would be quicker, so Peggy reluctantly acquiesced. Once in the car, it wasn't long before she was sitting back in her living room. There wasn't much to unpack. Just her toiletries and her clothes from the day before. It was Home Sweet Home again. But the silence was deafening.

Chapter 2

Biscuits, Barges and Booze

What started as a faint ticking from the grandmother clock in the passage grew progressively louder and more imposing. Each 'tock' signalling another lost moment seeping away from her existence; draining every sinew of emotion. A shipwrecked sailor, clinging on to life in a cold, lonely, unforgiving ocean of grief. Just when she thought that she had got into the swing of things, pangs of sadness would wash over her, leaving her so helpless that she would burst into tears. It had happened while shopping down at The Blue. It had even happened in the cinema last week, when she had gone with Pat and Babs to see a special screening of *It's a Wonderful Life*. How pathetic was that irony as she sat there staring at four walls? All she had left now was her memories. Her eyes flitted between pictures of her sisters with their husbands, her nephews, nieces and their children. None of her own children. They had tried, but it was never to be. Her gaze moved to a picture of her parents and other black and white pictures of her childhood, opening her mind like a Pandora's Box. Hope was now all she had.

"Them young people today wouldn't know pover'y if it bit them on the backside! They don't know the 'alf of it.

Bloody cheek, that bird callin' me 'common'. All 'igh and migh'y. All big 'at and no knickers." His speech was slurred. Almost incomprehensible. Her father's unsteady lurching gait betrayed a body and brain that were rather the worse for wear after a long drinking session with his friends at the *Colleen Bawn Arms* on a Friday night. Dad was right.

The life they had wasn't the life that anyone would understand today. The type of poverty in which they were raised was beyond explanation.

He would slump back in his armchair, a defiant look on his weather-beaten face, his arms folded. With that, he would promptly fall fast asleep, woken up only by a rumba on *Come Dancing* and then dragged to bed by his long-suffering wife, his arm draped around her shoulder. They were lucky to have a black and white telly. Most of her friends didn't. Only the children of Stevedores and some Lighterman children. Dad was a Deal Porter and earned a decent wage, but he loved his drink. He died young, in his early '50s. "It's the drink wot did it," her mother would say. "The doctor told 'im it'd kill him in the end. Stubborn man, your dad. But a good man with a good 'art."

It was now well past lunchtime. The cooker was barely used these days. It was ready meals in the evening and corn beef or tinned tuna sandwiches for lunch. There was no pleasure in cooking for one. Babs had asked her to think about Meals on Wheels. But she would get along just fine with meat and two veg from ready meals that she could heat in the microwave. She would sometimes treat herself with cod and chips from across the road, but it made the whole place stink of vinegar. After ferrying her plate back to the kitchen and returning to the sofa, she switched on the radio, just in time for *The Archers* but was soon up again to open the cabinet. The bottle was half empty. She had bought it only a few days before going into hospital. Strange that it seemed to get finished more quickly these days. Peggy poured out half a glass, the *glug, glug, glug* of the pale liquid fizzing like a mouthful of sherbet fountain expressing its delight in a splash of tonic water. The first sip bathed her body in a blanket of warmth, taking away the emotional pain of emptiness.

The second comforted a soul seeking solace and allowed her to slip back into the past once again.

Her mother and her 'Bermondsey Girls' as they liked to call themselves, were in their element. This time they had left the sitting room door open. She had grown strangely fond of this gathering, particularly being the only time that her mother could detach herself from the humdrum world of an endless cycle of cooking, cleaning and laundry.

"Now some say hopping's lousy
I don't believe it's true,
We only go down hopping
To earn a bob or two
With a tee-I-O, tee-I-ay, tee-I-ee-I-O."

All of them; Peggy, Pat, Babs, Mum and Dad would look forward to their annual hop picking trip. "'Opping's the poor people's holidee." Babs would giggle as she mimicked her teacher at Paradise Street Primary School.

They would spend the whole summer holidays hop picking. East Peckham in Kent was literally a breath of fresh air from the smoke and grime of Bermondsey. The whole family would be up by 4am, walk to London Bridge and take the Milk Train, pushing carts containing all their needs, including bedding. They picked hops from Monday to Friday and had weekends off. It was hard work, but there was such camaraderie and an idyllic rural life. Dad did most of the work. The children just moved the hops bin until it was full, and the tally man would arrive with his measuring basket. Now and again, the children would escape for a big adventure, sometimes scrumping apples and strawberries from farms around the hop fields.

The doorbell gave her a start.

"Coo-Eee! Peg!"

The letter box snapped shut again. Before Peggy had a chance to open the door, there was Babs.

"Pegs, luv. I 'eard you been at St Saviour's. They didn't half get you ou' quick. You've never been ill in yer life."

Peggy didn't have the heart to correct her. There had been that time when she was admitted with appendicitis. She recalled this vividly. There was no NHS then. She remembered her dad (who thought that he was out of earshot) telling her mother "Tha' cost me half a week's wages, tha' did." For all its faults, she appreciated the NHS. She really did. Babs had brought her some shopping from down The Blue.

After putting away the last egg in the fridge, Babs sat down in Jim's old chair. Peggy looked irritated.

"That's not your chair!" Her eyes welled up.

"Oh, Pegs. I'm sorry. I'm so sorry." Babs moved to comfort her sister, as she sobbed uncontrollably.

"I miss him. I miss my Jim. I miss my Jim." She reached for a tissue and Babs sat back down, this time next to her on the sofa.

"'Ow about I make you a nice cup'a'tea?"

Peggy followed her sister to the kitchen. "Babs. Please don't tell Pat. You know how she worries."

Her sobs were drowned out by the kettle that whistled as shrill as an exuberant station guard. Peggy was never one for electric kettles. Tea was meant to be made on the stove. A teapot and tea cosy were also prerequisites for a proper kitchen.

"'Course not, luv." Babs placed the teapot and two cups on a tray with a small bowl of sugar, two teaspoons, two custard creams and two digestives, manoeuvring the tray carefully as she negotiated the table and armchair in the lounge. Babs dunked a biscuit into her tea.

"Forget Dunkin' Donuts. This is even be'er. Dunkin' Digestives."

There was a pregnant pause, curtailed by uncontrollable fits of laughter from both sisters.

"D'yer remember Mum bringing back biscuits when she was at Peek Freans?"

Peggy nodded.

"We was so lucky when she used to bring back some to taste. Garibaldi with docker holes, Bourbon, chocolate tables, Marie and these." She pointed to the remaining biscuits on the tray. Peggy had fond memories of Mum walking with her sisters around the neighbourhood on a Saturday afternoon. You could smell the biscuits from outside the factory. A variety of smells emanating from the panoply of manufacturers could be anything from glue to leather to vinegar.

Over time, the factories had all disappeared. Peek Freans biscuits, Sarson's vinegar, Shuttleworth's chocolates, Crosse and Blackwell soup, Pink's and Hartley's jam, Pearce Duff's custard, Donkin's canning. The list could go on. She would never dare venture there at night these days. All that she heard about now was graffiti, burnt out cars and drug dealers. Most of the pubs had closed and people bought their booze from the supermarket or Off Licences. There were only two proper pie and mash shops left, with the other hot food coming from take-aways. Peggy no longer knew any of her immediate neighbours. They had either died or moved out in the '70s.

"It's all posh flats now." Peggy looked out of the net curtained window. "Woolies went years ago. We had butchers, bakers, greengrocers. Now its supermarkets where no one knows you. No one knows you anymore, Babs. No one knows you…"

"Gotta go now, Pegs." Babs scooped up her coat and kissed Peggy on what was still a slightly damp cheek.

"Gotta give Josie an 'and with the baby."

The door clicked shut. Peggy thought back to what she and Babs had talked about. Dad had a short life but some happy memories. Many's the time he would regale them with tales from the docks, with an embellishment that only Dad could pull off. All three would sit on the sofa on Sunday morning lapping up the tales of ships and barges, disappointed that they couldn't follow in his footsteps. But entranced by his knack of storytelling nonetheless. That is, on the rare occasions that he was in any fit state to tell them.

He was mostly either drunk on a Friday and Saturday night, or else sleeping it off the morning after. He was never violent with them. Only with Mum. All Pat and Babs remembered was him singing and talking loudly, before eventually dozing off to sleep in his chair.

Peggy's father, Cyril, came from a poor family. Working on the docks had been handed down the generations from time immemorial. Her grandfather was a run of the mill dock worker, but Cyril had worked his way up to become a Deal Porter. Friends and colleagues would joke about this and tease him mercilessly but in good humour, his surname being Lighterman. Workmates remarked that he had literally 'jumped ship' from his family roots of watermen, lightermen and bargemen.

"You know what they say about two short planks. You're be'er off 'ligh'ering," one of them once quipped. Cyril often referred to the Surrey Docks as the 'larder of London'. They had been established for over a century before Peggy was born. Although the London docks brought in all manner of commodities, Surrey Commercial Docks, as they were called, officially mainly imported timber from North America, Scandinavia and Russia. Soft wood was imported from Canada. The docks had shaped Bermondsey into the world that Peggy lived and breathed. There were eleven docks in all, but Cyril worked mainly at Canada Dock, a short walk from the Lighterman house. Like most of the men in Bermondsey at the time, Cyril became acculturated into the docks through working with his father. Unlike his father, he broke with tradition, moving away from barge work as a lighterman and became a deal porter. He still had to serve his time getting his licence as a freeman of the river but chose to specialise in the equally skilled profession of carrying and storing timber.

This could either be discharged into the water brought ashore by 'rafters' or else carried directly from ships that had docked. The docks were a closed shop where recognition and professional status was passed down generations, with the familiar question "'Oos boy are you then?" Deal porters carried roughly squared softwood or 'deal', which they stacked up to sixty feet high in warehouses. It was not for the faint-hearted, shifting long, heavy planks of wood day in, day out, was physically demanding and hazardous. Not only that, it needed manual dexterity and being fearless of heights.

Also known as 'Blondins' after the famous acrobat, deal porters wore what looked like leather bowler hats to which were attached long 'aprons' that draped over their shoulders to protect them from splinters. To carry and sometimes run with a pile of long slippery planks required tremendous hand-eye coordination and Cyril did it with aplomb. Come rain or shine, Cyril was out there, even in the damp and drizzly cloud of the pea-soupers.

His work was unpredictable. Although he rose early and had left the house by six in the morning, he could sometimes be gone for more than a day if piecework came up. This meant being given a fixed piece of work where it was the interest of the dockers to get it done as soon as possible. But hurrying the job was equally dangerous and could cost lives. A slip here or a trip there and that was it. Ships were also notoriously unpredictable in their arrival at the dockside, being slaves to the wind and the tide. Working conditions were a far cry from today's health and safety regulations. The air was often thick with smoke belched out by the ships and the warehouses were built at the turn of the century. They were squalid, with no lighting and often rat-infested. Sanitation was equally found wanting. Men would use a rotunda or large circular metal enclosure as a public urinal, better known as the Iron Lung.

As well as air pollution, water from the Thames contained waste from the gasworks, ironworks and from the sewers. The nature of their work meant that by the end of the day, the filth and grime from their travail would stay on their clothes and coat their faces and bodies. It was often the bus home that bore the brunt, meaning that the wealthy evening theatre goer may have to use that same seat at some stage that evening. Or you could shell out tuppence for a good scrub up at the local baths. If not, then a tin bucket and hot water at home. Getting a square meal at work just wasn't possible. Most dockers took their sandwiches to work under their caps, or else you could guarantee that they would be stolen or eaten by rats. If they wanted something more, they would rely on whatever the public house had to offer, which was pot luck as the pies were likely to be full of gristle. If you wanted something more up market like proper pie and mash or jellied eels, you'd have to venture further out of the docks. If you really wanted to put a spring in your step, there was nothing more invigorating then a Bombay oyster. Half a glass of vinegar with a raw egg dropped in it, sprinkled with pepper to boot.

There were times when the work was sparse, but woe betide you if illness or injury struck. The docking community and extended family would club together and donate a small weekly sum, but this was often slim pickings for the family in sustaining a decent standard of living. Which is why most dockers with nous would put a penny on the shelf, as it were, as fall-back money.

Cyril was luckier than many of his fellow dockers whose daily ritual was to stand around the foreman standing in the middle of the road, waiting for the call-on. Even then, there was plenty of pushing, punching and shoving to catch the eye of the gaffer. Those who weren't lucky enough that day would go down to Prescot Street where they relied on the offer of casual labour. After the war, for skilled docker workers such as stevedores, lightermen and deal porters, they would be paid if they didn't find work, as part of "bompin' on dabbin'". The equivalent of modern day 'signing-on'. Many dockers, both skilled and unskilled, made a habit of pilfering from ships for their families or for themselves, but Cyril frowned upon these 'mischievous blighters' who stole anything from peanuts to whiskey. He might have used different words to describe them if he was talking to his friends! But there was a code of conduct in the docks. If you were assigned to piecework for a 'dirty' job such as that involving coal or asbestos and you thought *Well, I don't quite fancy that, I'll go for another ship*, you could be in for a hefty fine. Cyril always said that the good humour and sense of belonging that he enjoyed at the docks was worth all the tea in China. But the lifestyle to which he had been accustomed was his downfall. It would perhaps not be surprising to hear that Cyril's nickname at work was 'Beano'. He was known for organising the annual trip down to the Margate, where literally hundreds of dockers would descend on this seaside town and return the same day more than a little beleaguered by booze.

Tragically, his nickname would be his death knell. That's where everything started to go downhill. In a worst possible way. Peggy's mum knew something was wrong when she would hear of dock gangers leaving Dad to sleep off his afternoon binge, 'roastin' on the stones'.

Peggy was the eldest of three. All born at home with two years between each of them. First her, then Pat, then Babs. Her earliest memory of Dad was telling her stories on a Sunday afternoon, with Babs and Pat looking on eagerly, although they were still only little nippers and just giggled or gasped when Peggy did. They copied her every expression – that is until they developed their own unique identities. And how different they were, and still were. But Dad was like Jekyll and Hyde. When he wasn't either drunk or recovering from a heavy session of drinking, which was usually on a Sunday morning, he wouldn't hurt a fly. He never lay a finger on the children, but Mum was scared of him. Really scared. She wouldn't dare utter a word when he came home blind drunk. Peggy only saw him hitting Mum once, but there were plenty more times unwitnessed. He came home not being able to string two words together and hit out when supper wasn't ready on time, but it wasn't long before Mum gave him a whack back with a rolling pin and then he thought twice before lashing out. That was a lesson he never forgot. Peggy wouldn't have been surprised if he fractured something, but he staggered to bed like a whimpering animal and never got himself checked out at St Olave's Hospital. After Cyril died, it all came out. As Peggy pieced together the puzzle of her father's drinking, she vowed that she would never be like him.

Cyril didn't talk much to Peggy about his early life, but his descriptions were hardly the tales of a nurturing and fulfilled childhood. His father, he would say, was a "bleedin' thug" who would drink heavily and often get home in a temper. In those days, it was customary for foreman to pay dockers' wages to the barman, who would take a set quota of four pints of beer from their wages, whether they drank it all up or not. They would often sit there late into the evening, many in silence, as they sipped their pints. It was then a long wait to be paid, sometimes in the early hours of the morning. He and his brother Ron knew that their father's return from the pub meant that it was 'time to scarper', often running for their lives. Even out of the downstairs window. His mother was frequently beaten black and blue but stayed with him. The children also fell foul of what his father referred to as "If they don't know 'ow to be'ave, I'll learn 'em."

His favourite weapon of choice was the belt. Sometimes Cyril wouldn't be able to sit down at school without the stinging making him wince. The funny thing was, Peggy and her sisters never knew their grandad's name. It was as like saying "The Scottish Play" in case it brought a curse on the Lighterman family. Cyril's dad died young, in his 40s, from pneumonia. Marj suspected that it was something to do with the asbestos that he worked with, but the doctors couldn't be certain. Cyril had his first taste of alcohol when he was ten. His father had come home with a bottle that he had pilfered from the docks and insisted that it wouldn't do the children any harm to have a drop of rum. He remembered it burning his throat, but his father just laughed, joking that it "It'll make a man of you."

Cyril started drinking regularly in his late teens, largely at the behest of his peer group, who, like him, were all dockers acculturated into the life of a drink before breakfast, a drink at lunchtime and then again after the working day was done. That was a fair whack of booze, amounting to over six pints of beer per day or twelve units of alcohol in today's money. It didn't take long before alcohol took its toll. Peggy often remembered him feeling sick in the morning, which often woke her up at some unearthly hour. If it wasn't that, he would sometimes clutch his tummy, just under the right side of his rib cage and be off work for a few days. He never told the doctor, even when he had bouts of pain and swelling in his toes. When Peggy left school to train as a teacher, he had already started to suffer the consequences. Each year that passed saw a demise that she was powerless to prevent. He would fly into a rage if his family or friends would comment on his drinking. He would often be doubled up in pain when he got an inflamed liver. Even on the rare occasions that the doctor was called by Mum to see him, he would swear his head off, leaving the doctor's entry simply to record "I attempted to examine Mr Lighterman's abdomen, but he was far from polite." When Peggy got engaged to Jim, they would hear of his frequent arguments at work with the foreman, getting into work late and getting into scraps with colleagues over the slightest peccadillo. It was only when he approached his late 40s, that they started to notice that Cyril was to show a yellowish hue and the doctors had warned him that he had cirrhosis and that he was playing with his life.

But he was past the point of no return and spent three months at St Olave's Hospital, in his last days, clinging onto dear life before sinking into a coma. That was it. The booze had finished him off. He wasn't the first to have reaped the hazards of the demon brew. His own father had gone the same way, no doubt; it probably wasn't just the asbestos. It was something almost taken for granted in the docks. The price you paid for the job that you did and company you kept. It was as if the curtain had come down on Act One of the Lighterman story. But Peggy still had Mum, her sisters and the love of her life, Jim.

Chapter 3

When Jim Died

"Ooh, that bloke over there ain't half dishy."

The Christmas Lightermans Dance was in full swing on a crisp and even December evening in 1950. Babs had a cheeky grin on her face, as she pointed to a tall, slim man in the corner, sitting on his own staring into the distance with a lemon cordial grasped gingerly in his right hand.

"What d'yer think, Pegs? 'Ees got his eye on you. I just know it."

A crimson shade of red flushed across Peggy's face. Slowly, she turned her head towards the person of interest. He was certainly a head turner, but she'd never so much as looked at a man before this rite of passage into womanhood. Sweet sixteen and never been kissed. And that's the way she wanted it to stay until she got a steady job. She felt a wave of goose bumps as she caught his eye. Both looked away sharply, but neither made the first move until Babs grabbed Peggy by her hand and dragged her towards a young man who looked a startled rabbit standing in front of a fast-approaching car with its headlights on full beam. Babs plonked her sister in a nearby seat and beat a hasty retreat. "'Ow d'yer do" was the first social overture that Jim could muster.

"I'm fine, thank you." Peggy felt strangely relaxed and felt an immediate connection. As the evening progressed, they had agreed that another meeting would be mutually agreeable. She had found him a good laugh and charming. He had found her beautiful and softly spoken.

Peggy imagined that the bravado of his peer group would mean that their encounter would be described with a degree of hyperbole and probably much coarser language! Nevertheless, their relationship blossomed, and they were soon seeing each other more regularly.

Jim's father had been killed on the docks during the War. On 7 September 1940, nearly half of the eight hundred and forty-three attacks by the German Luftwaffe were in Bermondsey. The attacks lasted for fifty-seven of the next fifty-eight days. Jim was only ten when the war broke out and was evacuated to Dorset. Returning to find that his father had died was heart breaking. The docks never slept, even during the relentless shelling. His mother had brought him and his four siblings up with the help of their extended family, but his mother was compelled to take up a job at Peek Freans Biscuit Factory to help make ends meet. He doted on his mother, whom he described as 'an angel'. By the time Peggy had started courting Jim, she was still living in Bermondsey but had moved to work at Crosse and Blackwell. The five years' age difference between them didn't faze Peggy but he wondered if she treated him more a like a father figure. Whenever they had a tiff, she would tell him "Dad would never have said that", knowing full well that Jim was a more sensitive and gentler being than her own father.

Jim had excelled at his trade, becoming a Stevedore working mainly at Millwall Docks. He had been subject to the usual trials and tribulations of a docker's life but had perhaps surprisingly not engaged fully in the drinking culture to which many dockers were inevitably drawn. In some ways, his fellow dockers had regarded him as somewhat of a misfit. Instead of a swift couple of pints at the *Ship Aground*, he would rather go home and listen to the wireless. Combined with an engaging manner and often somewhat unsure of himself, he was altogether a good egg to whom Peggy was irresistibly drawn.

The first time she went to the pictures was a very special moment in Peggy's life, sitting in the back row of the Troc-Ette cinema on Tower Bridge Road, after pie and mash with parsley liquor and jellied eels on the side. Jim had saved up all month to take her out to see *The Moon is Blue*. He was a true gentleman, only holding her hand once, for a moment.

Their first kiss was not until a few months later. Days became weeks, became years and it was time for Jim to do the honourable thing. They married when she had finished teacher training. She was 20. But they didn't move from Peggy's mum's until much later. Moving into their own flat was a new experience and finding one was no problem, as being from Bermondsey meant their automatic entitlement to social housing. It was just down the road from both mothers-in-law.

A far cry from Peggy and Jim's childhoods, with an inside bathroom and toilet and small black and white telly. As they lived through the domestic revolution in household appliances, they went from twin tub to washing machine; from dustpan and brush to vacuum cleaner; from wood burner to central heating. They had even reached the dizzy heights of satellite TV and mobile phones in the last few years of their precious life together. First, they lived with Peggy's mum and later moved to Bellamy Estate, where they literally knew everyone on the sprawling urban complex. The whole community was devastated when its fate was sealed, after which the couple moved to the thirteenth floor of an even larger complex as part of the Chuzzlewit Estate. Jim continued to work on the docks during the early part of their marriage, but change took its course, as change always does. The advent of the freight container had taken the movement of goods to a different level and the moving and handling of goods by hand was no longer needed.

When the Surrey docks closed in the early 1970s, Jim was given the choice of working further afield in Tilbury but turned it down. He was still barely forty, still fit and active and managed to secure a job as porter at St Saviour's Hospital. Bermondsey hadn't been the same since the second World War. Although largely flattened and re-built, many had moved away, as they continued to do in the 1960s and '70s. Pubs were now flats, high street butchers, bakers and grocers now take-aways.

The large thriving markets at Tower Bridge and down The Blue were shadows of their former selves. At least The Lane was still busy and within walking distance from the Bellamy. It was where Peggy went for her fruit and veg, as well as picking up other bargains along the way. After a few years of marriage, they were resigned to their fate of being childless and Peggy treated Pat and Babs' children like her own. How they loved to come for tea to Auntie Peggy and Uncle Jim, where they would be thoroughly spoilt with cake and squash.

Jim's 70th birthday was celebrated with style. It seemed as if the whole of south east London had congregated in the modestly sized church hall. He had always worn his Sunday best, even after his retirement five years previously. Forever the dapper gentleman, but with a vice for what he would laugh off as 'cancer sticks'. On this occasion, it was a Cuban cigar bought by Peggy's mum. Times had changed with smoke free regulations and he would need to enjoy it outside. It was while taking one of the numerous puffs that he would take that afternoon, that Peggy noticed his suit looked looser on him. She hadn't seen him wear it since they went out on her birthday, but he had most certainly lost weight. Jim was a bon viveur, always fond of his food and Marj said that he could "eat for England." But something wasn't right.

A few months later, on a rare trip to the West End to buy Peggy's mum a birthday present, Jim began to cough uncontrollably.

Peggy had been used to his coughing fits. The doctor had diagnosed him with emphysema and 'COPD'. This was different. They had to stop and sit down, such was the length of this bout. At this point, on bringing out his handkerchief and coughing into it, Peggy noticed specks of blood on Jim's hand. It all happened so fast. First the consultations, then the scans and blood tests, before the inevitable news that it was cancer. Peggy would often wake up at night with panic attacks, checking to see if Jim was still breathing. He became frailer and more cachectic, augmented by chemo and radiotherapy but the former made him weak and sick. He had aged twenty years in just a few months. Very soon, it was time to start preparing for the worst. Jim was admitted to a hospice to live out his last few weeks.

There was something incredibly serene about the atmosphere at St Christ's Hospice. All the staff were calm, polite and it was everything that she could have wished for, but it was still difficult to see a road ahead in a life without Jim. They had done everything together and Peggy had lost contact with most of her friends over the months as Jim's full-time carer. It was a thirty-minute bus ride but she visited him twice a day, staying for two hours at a time.

In the final few days, she stayed for progressively longer and stayed the night when she knew that he had given up the fight. The first day that Peggy visited him at St Christ's Hospice, she arrived late. Having to take two buses to site some five miles away in rush hour and school run time meant being unable to board the first and second buses from being jam packed. When she finally arrived, out of breath and a little dishevelled from the blustery morning, she could barely catch her breath as she made a beeline for the nursing station. She sat there for a few moments talking to the nurse about Jim's care. Unlike the hustle and bustle of St Saviour's Hospital, the nurses had time to sit and talk, explaining in detail about Jim's care. She spoke about how the team would manage problems such as pain, bowels, eating and drinking, and how they would avoid problems such as chest and urine infections by getting Jim out of bed during the day. If there was ever such a thing, she hoped that it would be a 'good death'. They would also make sure that managing his personal care such as washing, dressing, feeding and toileting was done with dignity and privacy. Jim had his own room. It was spacious, warm and decorated with paintings. Peggy had brought in some pictures to instil a feeling of familiarity. She kept their wedding photo in a suitable place within Jim's eyeline.

The bed was specially adapted, with a ripple mattress and elaborate controls that allowed different seating positions.

Peggy felt helpless seeing Jim lie there, his face almost ashen, with an oxygen mask, gasping for breath. With a sudden resurrection of emotion, Jim took off his mask and opened his arms for a hug. As they embraced, Peggy let out an outpouring of anguish, as she told him how she missed him and how she would always love him. Jim started to well up but tried to contain his emotions as he tried to make this moment last forever. For the next few hours, interrupted by lunch and nursing observations, Peggy spoke, and Jim listened. She was not one for talking nor one for awkward silence. Never had she spoken so much about some much of their life together.

The consultant and the whole palliative care team had been simply wonderful, paying close attention to Jim's wishes, which could be anything from his choice of food to the music that he enjoyed. She had never heard of Advanced Care Planning when Dad was alive. Jim wanted to be cremated and his ashes scattered in the Thames, near Canada Dock. He didn't want an elaborate funeral, with only his brother's and Peggy's immediate family and some of his old docker friends invited to the Service, which he wanted to be held at St Julian's Church.

It was the day that Peggy had been dreading. She was called early in the morning by the Hospice to say that Jim was becoming agitated and that they were now at the stage where they were administering medication to ease the restlessness. Peggy was there in a heartbeat. She had a reliable taxi company that she had used in emergencies. When she arrived, Jim was restless, trying to remove his drip but became immediately calmer when Peggy held his hand and whispered in his ear.

"Is that you, Mum?" he said in a muffled tone behind the oxygen mask.

"Jim, it's me, Peggy." Peggy could not understand how he could mistake her for his own mother. Jim began to talk incomprehensibly.

There would be just words and then just phrases, none of which connected with each other in any meaningful order. Over the next few hours, he drifted in and out of consciousness, until becoming progressively drowsier. All this time, he held tightly onto Peggy's hand, like a child on his first day of school. He started breathing erratically. "Agonal breathing," the nurse later explained, signifying the very last gasps. Jim became still. So still. The hand that had formed an indelible bond for life became suddenly limp. It was over. She had loved him with all her heart and now he was gone. Jim was gone. As she looked upon that lifeless body, Peggy's heart was broken.

She knew that no matter how long she remained on this earth, it would never mend completely. After losing Jim, a part of her had also died. She also felt lifeless. A drifting soul. A fallen woman.

Chapter 4

The Secret

15.09.2003

Dear Doctor Hither,

I would be grateful if you could see Mrs Peggy Lighterman, a 70-year-old widow whose husband died from lung cancer last year. She had a recent overnight admission to St Saviour's Hospital, following a fall. There was no head injury sustained and no evidence of bony injury. Since her discharge, she has presented to the surgery nearly every 2 weeks for the past 6 months, complaining of a variety of problems, all non-specific in nature. These include feeling sick, sleeping poorly and complaining of dizziness. She has had extensive investigations by the care of the elderly, neurology and gastroenterology teams, but there has been no physical cause found for her symptoms.

Apart from a history of hypertension and acid reflux, there is no other relevant past medical history. She has strong family support from her sisters and is independent with all activities of daily living. I wondered whether she might have depression but would value your opinion.

Yours Sincerely
Dr Arnold Moorse

Dr Hither scanned the referral closely. It was not by any means unusual for an older person with depression to present in such a manner, particularly given the stigma associated with mental illness and the need to report physical manifestations of depression. This generation was told to 'pull your socks up', with a 'keep calm and carry on' ethos where showing your feelings represented a sign of weakness or moral failing. It was seen as a character flaw that was swept under carpet if you were to admit to being a 'depressive'. He booked a home visit for the following week.

Dr Hither had worked in Bermondsey for many years as a community psychiatrist. He was indeed fortunate to be working in a community mental health team that valued considering patients as part of their community and families, rather than just illnesses to be treated. He also valued something that he had never previously seen. The relentless dedication and commitment of Bermondsey families in caring for their loved ones in this tightly knit community that he affectionately called a 'riverside village'. Such was the strength of these bonds, he would frequently find relatives with their own families travelling from a place several miles away, sometimes twice a week, just to provide practical and emotional support. This could be shopping, collecting medicines or accompanying to hospital appointments. There was something very special about the strong sense of community.

But it is one that had become increasingly fragmented, with only small pockets remaining where older people still knew their neighbours. Those who had replaced them were often out at work all day, meaning that older people who still lived there didn't see anyone other than their families from one week to the next. He often reflected on his own childhood around a similar council estate over forty years previously. In fact, his own upbringing during early childhood was probably more 'working class' than many of his colleagues. What had struck him most was that the hand you are dealt in life shapes the rest if your life. He had seen what it meant not just to live modestly but be stuck on a hamster wheel of deprivation and despair where peer pressure and lack or parental supervision can so easily mean that opportunities are missed. In the worst cases, it could also mean children developing problems with drug and alcohol or being involved with crime. Yes, he wasn't the butter wouldn't melt in his mouth angel. He had been dared to go and ring doorbells and run away as fast as his legs could carry him. To be caught smoking by his parents at the age of nine. To accidentally break the neighbour's window with the football and feign ignorance. But his parents had appreciated the value of education and so he moved in a very different direction to his friends. In fact, when he started studying in earnest, all his 'working class' friends deserted him for being a 'swot'.

He would later hear of childhood chums from the neighbourhood taking drugs or ending up in prison. It was the harsh reality of social deprivation. Any new challenges that he faced as a psychiatrist just paled into insignificance when he considered the challenges faced by his patients. They had never been given the chance to pull themselves out of the quicksand of ill health and he was going to make jolly sure that he would never ever give up on them. Perhaps, unconsciously, Dr Hither may have even considered himself a modern-day Alfred Salter. What he most admired about the sometimes hostile, and sometimes distant population that he found himself serving was their plain warts and all honesty. There was no hiding behind a clever cliché or oxymoron. They were as you saw them. If they didn't like what you said, they would tell you. It didn't matter how many letters you had after your name or whether you spoke with received pronunciation. It did matter that you treated them with just the same respect that you showed anyone else.

But it also mattered to Dr Hither that the men and women of Bermondsey would often not ask for help when they needed it. This meant advocating for them even more strongly. It was this sense of natural social justice that Dr Hither valued most. It was not about just doing things right. It was about doing the right thing.

The bus was mostly empty, save for a handful of people. Par for the course on a weekday morning. Schools had broken up for summer. It was the usual mix of travellers. Tourists (often families or couples), sitting at the front to obtain a ringside view of Tower Bridge before alighting at Druid Street, with one or other parent clutching a map intently, pointing vigorously in several directions before choosing a preferred collective direction. Mothers with babies in buggies, pushing with one hand, the other trying to entice another crying child onto the bus. Placing the buggy in the middle of the bus and darting to the front to swipe a payment card against the beeping sensor. Older people, some bent double, carrying heavy shopping. Weighed down by groceries and some by life. But today, none of the school children were pushing, shoving, jostling, chuckling as they messily devoured their breakfast of chicken and chips and discarded the empty box in some dusty shop doorway.

Londoners, especially those from around the area, were not ones for keeping their thoughts and emotions to themselves. "Is this bus moving any time soon, driver?"

The driver had stopped for longer than usual. His protracted stay followed the all-too-familiar automated message. "This bus will wait at this stop for three minutes to even out the service."

One irate traveller scurried down the stairs and leapt out of the open door, shaking his head vigorously. "Bloody disgrace. London Buses."

Dr Hither's experience with home visits by bus had resulted in a large helping of empathy for the plight of bus drivers. But most were grateful, using the customary "Thank you, driver" or saluting as they alighted. Others were simply ungrateful, no matter what the efforts were of the driver to placate them. Bus stops in London were mostly fewer than a couple of minutes apart and the next took longer than expected. A muffled merry-go-round melody heralded the appearance of a ramp, offering safe passage to a wheelchair user and her helper. "The next bus stop is closed." Dr Hither was sure that the lady who spoke on his Sat-Nav bore a striking resemblance to these dulcet tones.

"Bermondsey Parade two fousand and free."

Dr Hither looked up, startled by the distraction.

"C'mon you stupid machine. I said Bermondsey Parade."

A man wearing a black retro donkey jacket, a can of energy drink in one hand and mobile tablet telephone in the other, was attempting to engage the listening software. But it wasn't playing ball.

"Right. Last time," he muttered, in sheer desperation. "Ber Mond Sey Pa Rade two fousand and free."

"Yeah, got it. Get in!"

He showed the results of his endeavours to a fellow passenger, displaying a web page on his tablet screen with details of the annual parade that he had been attending since a small child. Finally, it seemed that all was right with the world.

Dr Hither was already running late, thanks to the shenanigans of London Transport, but then came the last straw. "This bus is on diversion. Please listen carefully for further announcements."

The imperfect start to another life in the day of a doctor in the house. Apart from a slightly longer walk because of roadworks at the planned stop, the journey to Peggy's flat was straightforward. In fact, Dr Hither could guarantee that over half his patients lived either off the Walworth Road or off The Blue.

Once there, the concrete jungle was difficult to navigate. Post codes and online maps were all well and good, but the imposing tower blocks were difficult to differentiate from one another. It felt so easy to be forgotten in this post-war urban wilderness. After walking around in a circuitous fashion, Dr Hither finally came upon a large board outlining the layout of the estate, with a 'You are here' arrow marked in faded green.

Each building had its own entrance for clusters of flats, resulting in a more protracted journey to the intended destination on the Chuzzlewit Estate.

Once at the front entrance, he pressed the call button, to be greeted with an announcement reminiscent of a train arriving at a station.

"Calling seventy, eight...please wait." There was no verbal response, but the door buzzer sounded and Dr Hither grabbed the handle, heaving the heavy metal door to. At last, he was in. The doors of the lift were sprayed with multi-coloured graffiti in the style of the artist. He pressed the cold plastic button to summon the mobile metal box. The floors lit up on the screen above the lift.

17...15...13...After much clunking and whirring, the lift doors opened slowly. There was no indication as to which floor corresponded to which flat number, so it was pure guesswork. Trial and error. After getting out at the wrong floor, looking the numbers listed on the wall and walking up and down flights of stairs, the correct floor revealed itself. He was fifteen minutes late. It was an occupational hazard of home visits, especially on large estates. A large iron grill lay across the front door. The bell chime could be heard from outside. Dr Hither was a little rusty on the tune but it sounded like an up-tempo version of *Eine Kleine Nachtmusik.* The security chain unloosened, the door opened, sticking a little as it did so.

Peggy was a thin lady of average height with dyed blonde hair in a bob, wearing a blue tie dye top, jeans and a coral necklace. She had always taken pride in her appearance, but had made an extra special effort, just to prove that she was coping. A stark contrast to how she was feeling inside.

"Sorry, Doctor, it's not as clean as I'd like it to be." Peggy's apologetic tone surprised Doctor Hither, as he looked around what appeared to be a flat in pristine condition. The kitchen was spotless, with all surfaces squeaky clean, a small cactus plant adorning the window sill and several 'Happy 70th' birthday cards decorating the top of the fridge. Dishcloths were neatly folded; the chrome kitchen sink was wiped clean and a breadbin and toaster were out on the worktop. The washing machine was on its spin cycle, as he was shown to the lounge. As Peggy was making a cup of tea for her visitor, an offer that he found not uncommon among people living in this area, he had chance to glance around, as he prepared for the interview.

The lounge window offered a view of other high-rise blocks looming large over the Elephant and Castle skyline, frozen in time since the 1960s. Aside from various ornaments and a carriage clock, the mantelpiece was lined with pictures of the Lighterman family. There was Mum and Dad's wedding picture, pictures of Peggy and her sisters at different ages and a large gold framed picture of Peggy and Jim taken the year before, on holiday in Tenerife. A garden had been created in the limited space available on her balcony. It was Peggy's pride and joy. She insisted that she show Dr Hither the fruits of her labour, even though she hadn't been doing as much to maintain it of late.

Every colour of the rainbow was on display. Petunias, begonias and geraniums arranged in pots. Fuchsias in hanging baskets. Pansies, marigolds and sweet alyssum in window boxes. She waxed lyrical about the garden that she used to have before moving to her current flat, showing Dr Hither faded pictures taken in polaroid. Buddleia, hydrangea, lavender in flower beds. Roses of different shapes and sizes – climbing, floribunda and hybrid tea. Even jasmine and honeysuckle. No space unfilled. It was a mesmerising display of visual artistry and sensory delight. They returned to the cool of the flat.

"Here you are, Doctor. Tea with milk and one sugar. Let me know if you need more milk."

After a customary initial sip, Dr Hither started the interview.

"I'm not mad, Doctor, if that's what you think."

Peggy's only knowledge of Psychiatry came from the big screen. Skin crawling portrayals of 'mentally deranged, knife-wielding schizos' that had preyed on Peggy's innermost fears of what it was like to be 'mental'. Hers was the not the Psychiatry of the twenty-first century, it was one of Norman Bates and Hannibal Lecter. Films such as *One Flew Over the Cuckoo's Nest* and *The Shining* had misled generations into believing the myth of the 'split personality' and that people with mental illness were dangerous and not to be trusted.

Doctor Hither had been well accustomed to his patients being under the automatic assumption that he was there to 'certify' them and take them forcibly to 'funny farm' or 'workhouse'. After reassuring Peggy that the whole purpose of visit was to see how his team could keep her living at home independently for as long as possible, the drawbridge on Peggy's preconceptions slowly came down.

"What should I call you? Mrs Lighterman? Peggy?"

Peggy remembered how flippant she'd been with the doctor after her fall. She owed it to herself to treat this interview with that bit more respect.

"Peggy is fine. Thank you, Doctor."

She gave Dr Hither her full attention as he started scribbling his notes. Scribbling was the word all right. It seemed true enough what they said about doctors' writing.

"Oh, and Doctor, I got this letter from the hospital. I can't make head nor tail of it, Doctor. Please tell me what it means."

The crumpled sheet was thrust into Dr Hither's expert hand. The print was so small, it was barely readable. But the jargon. Oh, the jargon! The Greek. The Latin. A language of its own that was not designed to be understood by anyone other than doctors. Dr Hither went through each of the medical terms, acronyms and abbreviations with painstaking patience. BIBA-brought in by ambulance. PC-presenting complaint. That was just the first two lines.

Then there was HT-hypertension. GORD-gastro-oesophageal reflux disease and CKD-chronic kidney disease. The medication was as much of a mouthful. BD-Latin for twice a day. By the end, Dr Hither felt as if he was back in medical school. Although he did recall some acronyms that only medical students could devise. There was NAD, which was supposed to mean No Abnormality Detected. For medical students attempting to blag their way through presenting a case, it meant Not Actually Done. But the crowning glory had to be awarded to an interpretation of one of the longest medical terms. The tongue twister of medical procedures. Endoscopic Retrograde Cholangio Pancreatogram or ERCP was translated as Emergency Retrograde Clerking of Patients. The miscreant medical students who couldn't be bothered to see the patient themselves would cheekily copy the clerking done by the junior doctor and pass it off as their own. Though it didn't take long before said student was rumbled when the consultant delved into more detail about their findings. It was a technique that such students would rarely employ more than once. Peggy seemed content with the medical tutorial.

"So, Peggy…your GP asked me to see you because she was worried about how you were feeling, and I know that you have lost your husband recently."

"It seemed as if everything happened so quickly." Her voice became tremulous. "Jim died and suddenly everyone was there. As soon as the funeral was over, they all just vanished.

"I mean…don't get me wrong, Doctor, Pat and Babs are gems. I can always count on them if I need them. But I seem to just push them away. Now it seems as if I'm just going through the motions of living. One day is just as much the same as another. I feel better when I go out and I'm around people. But as soon as that door shuts and I'm on my own, it feels as if time has stopped."

Dr Hither leaned forward a little but remained silent. It was clear that he was actively listening.

"I still keep his things just the way he left them…and I often talk to his picture. I even thought I could feel his presence just after he died and…and…"

Tears began to flow. Dr Hither offered her a tissue from the box on the table.

"I even saw him sitting in the chair once at night. Does that mean I'm going mad, Doctor? Please don't take me away. Please…"

Dr Hither broke his silence.

"Peggy. Most people who have lost a loved one will have experiences like the ones that you've described. They are all part of the grieving process…"

Peggy looked reassured.

"…I can't imagine it's been easy for you…" he continued, his tone calm and reassuring. "How is your appetite?"

"I just don't have the taste for food anymore."

"Have you lost any weight?"

"Well, I never used to be this thin."

"What about your clothes? Do they feel looser on you?"

"I used to be a 12. Look at me now." She patted her tummy. "I'm an 8 now."

"Tell me about your sleep."

"I'm not sleeping well at all, Doctor. I can't seem to get to sleep. I just lie there, staring into space. Even if I do sleep, I only get a few hours and wake up feeling horrible. Horrible!"

"What is a typical day like for you now?" Doctor Hither was keen to establish how all these problems had affected Peggy's routine and the quality of her life.

"It's so easy just to lie there, Doctor. I lie there all day, with the duvet pulled over my head. I don't reply to any messages. Don't check the post. Don't do anything really. I force myself to eat, to get dressed, to get washed. It feels like I'm wading through treacle."

Dr Hither tried to leave no stone unturned in covering all the areas necessary to carry out a thorough assessment. He then finished off with by testing Peggy's memory.

"Would you mind if I ask you some questions about your memory?"

He'd heard it all, from "Don't ask me such childish questions" to "Why I should be bothered about that. I don't take much notice of what day or date it is". He knew that when patients gave the latter reply, it was often a way of rationalising their deteriorating memory.

"What year is it?"

"2003."

"And the month?"

"July."

And so, it continued, until the end of an interview that had lasted well over an hour.

"Oh, Doctor. I'm sorry. I didn't offer you another cuppa."

If there was one thing that the spirit of Bermondsey had imprinted on Dr Hither, it was the hospitality.

"That's all right, Peggy, very kind of you to offer, but I'm fine."

"So, I'm not losing my marbles then, Doctor?" she exclaimed, equating the assessment with an attempt to assess her for 'Alzheimer's'. She knew very well the devastation caused to the lives of people with dementia and had a vivid recollection of visiting her Uncle Henry in a Home.

He would repeat the same thing again and again, not recognise Mum and get angry with the staff. That was not definitely not going to be her.

Dr Hither explained that his assessment pointed to a diagnosis of depression. Peggy knew that something was wrong, but depression? She reluctantly accepted the diagnosis and agreed to start treatment with depression tablets. She called them 'happy pills'. When offered talking therapy, she declined, stating that she would rather talk to Dr Hither and see whether she felt better with tablets. Peggy had successfully evaded the subject of her drinking. Just as in hospital, there was an automatic assumption that women of her age probably don't drink. And if they do, it would probably be the 'odd sherry' on social occasions. They probably think that drinking's good for you. That's what the Toucan said on the ad when she was a child! As soon as Dr

Hither had left, Peggy poured herself her second drink of the day. What started as something to blot out the pain and heartache after Jim died had now become something of a habit. She never had the taste for it before, but it made her feel relaxed and numbed her senses like an emotional painkiller. She had some gin left over from last summer, when she had a gin and tonic to celebrate Pat's birthday. She couldn't stomach the taste of beer and the tonic made the gin more palatable. It was her treat. After all, it was her only pleasure. Maybe she shouldn't have had that second glass before she fell and had to be admitted to hospital. But it wasn't that.

She'd just got up too quickly, that's all. What's the harm in a small drink now and again? The problem was that now and again had turned into twice a day.

She hadn't even considered the possibility of her drinking being a problem, even though she had started to feel sick and dizzy. The doctors had found nothing. No one had even asked her. It was her own business and that was that.

Peggy tried to lead as normal a life as possible but found herself doing less and less with her day. Even after Jim died, she still spent most of the day out of house. Either shopping or visiting her sisters. But everything seemed to change imperceptibly. Her drinking had crept up on her, but instead of tapping her on the shoulder, it had hung over her like a dark cloud. She now made do with tinned food and ready-made meals. After her last drink at night, she would often fall asleep in front of the television. She hadn't taken the tablets that Dr Hither had prescribed, because she was worried that they might make her feel worse if she was drinking. She couldn't look her drinking in the eye, but it continued to devour her in a way that she could never have imagined.

Dr Hither visited Peggy again at home a month later. This time he found a very different patient sitting talking to him in a room that was considerably more cluttered than before. The kitchen was not its usual immaculate self, with unwashed plates and bowls in the sink.

Peggy was still in her nightdress at ten o'clock in the morning, her hair uncombed and looking down at the floor.

"I'm so sorry that you have to see me like this, Doctor. I'm trying my best, but nothing's working. Nothing…I really don't see the point in living like this. I'd be better off dead. Who would care anyway? Sometimes, I wish I'd go to sleep and never wake up."

Peggy looked even thinner than before. Her gesture and speech were so slowed down, with long pauses between each sentence. It was clear that Peggy wasn't coping, and that her mental state had deteriorated to such an extent that even she admitted she needed help. She agreed to being admitted to a mental health inpatient unit. Dr Hither explained that it probably wouldn't be a long admission and that it was mainly to assess to see what other treatment could be offered. Peggy called Pat, who drove her to the hospital, both viewing the admission with some trepidation. A large plastic sign greeted them above the door. 'Welcome to Ada Salter Ward'. Now that was a name that Peggy recognised. A household name in Bermondsey. Ada, and her husband Dr Alfred Salter, had never been forgotten in Bermondsey. Both social reformers who had dedicated their lives to improving the wellbeing of every resident with a selflessness that was both rare and humbling. As MP and GP, they had left a legacy. It was thanks to Ada Salter that Bermondsey had a solarium and public baths as far back as the 1930s.

The ward was different. No open plan design with bays and central observation point. No patients confined to bed with beeping and buzzing equipment. It seemed more tranquil. Peggy had her own room.

A little sparse, but the opportunity to bring in her own possessions to provide a sense of comfort and familiarity. Pat sat with her on the bed.

"Peggy, luv. It's for the best. Don't you worry, I'll come and see you every day. They'll look after you fine. I'm sure they will." Pat didn't stay for long and supper was served shortly after.

"No pie and mash here, I don't suppose?" Peggy asked the nurse serving the patients. Even in her darkest hour, Peggy tried to keep her spirits up.

"No, Peggy, but we do a mean cod and chips on a Friday." She winked, as she put down a plate of cauliflower cheese, broccoli and roast potatoes.

Peggy was starting to feel a little brighter. She also felt surprisingly hungry. By the time she had finished her supper, her plate was empty. The admitting doctor saw her. The same questions as Dr Hither had asked her, give or take. But she didn't have the wherewithal to go through the memory test yet again and politely declined. The doctor also performed a physical examination. No surprises there. She had been used to being poked around when she was in Patience Ward.

After blood was taken, she took her evening medication and hoped for a better night's sleep. She slept better. Surprisingly well, in fact.

The next morning, she awoke feeling refreshed and her head was clear. Peggy hadn't felt this well for a long time. The only difference was that she wasn't drinking. But it never entered her mind for a minute that this was anything whatsoever connected with her new lease of life. It was Dr Hither's ward round day. But before Peggy, there were several other patients that needed to be seen.

Derek had vascular dementia. He was active and independent before his first stroke a year ago. Apart from problems with speech and walking, he'd shown a profound change in his personality. A retired judge, he transformed from a mild-mannered man to someone almost unrecognisable to family and friends. His language was coarse, with frequent use of expletives; his behaviour impulsive and his judgement impaired. Before admission to Ada Salter Ward, he had ordered £5000 worth of 'presents' for his family from a mail order catalogue. He had also been aggressive to carers and his wife. There were several decisions to be made, not least of which was whether it would be in his best interest to return home with the same care package and risk being back to square one.

June had schizophrenia. She had gone to her GP some months before, reporting that neighbours were coming into her house and stealing her food. She also believed that they had planted recording devices in her attic and always knew exactly which room she was in. She was sure that she could hear them talk to each other and discuss her, as well as give a running commentary on what she was doing. On the ward, she believed that her food was being poisoned. That was just two patients on a ward of fifteen. Each with their own problems.

Suspicious, angry, frightened, perplexed. Psychiatry wasn't just about treating their symptoms. It was about considering them as part of a relationship. A relationship with society. It was about offering hope. A better quality of life. A life worth living.

Through all his professional trials and tribulations, it's why Dr Hither chose Psychiatry. Perhaps one of the most challenging but rewarding professions. How do you de-escalate a situation involving a patient who is acutely agitated and aggressive, with little insight into their behaviour? How do you offer solace to patient who is suicidal and believes that they are evil, wicked and deserve to die? It's what Psychiatrists live and breathe as part of their working lives. Making small improvements can mean big changes in people's lives. It can also save lives. But Peggy had continued to elude the medical profession.

It seemed an obvious question to ask but so far, no doctor or nurse had any inkling about her drinking. She was in denial and that was the way it was probably always going to be. If this charade continued, Peggy was only fooling one person. Peggy Lighterman. A few days into her admission, Peggy appeared to have made a miraculous discovery. Perhaps the antidepressants had worked and that this had coincided with her admission. But Dr Hither was left scratching his head. Something didn't seem right.

As soon as Peggy returned home on a hot and humid July afternoon, she opened the windows to clear the musty aroma of loneliness, then straight to the cabinet to pour herself a large gin and tonic.

She'd craved a drink in hospital and was relieved to experience the immediate feeling of relaxation from her 'friend in a bottle' as she called it. But nothing had changed. She had gone straight back to square one. The problem was no longer the loss of Jim; it was now the loss of Peggy.

Chapter 5

The Resistance

The sultry sunny days all merged into one as Peggy's life became frozen in time, the long July evenings spent gazing over a hazy skyline that felt as empty as she did. She lived off tea and biscuits, with the occasional take-away (often half eaten) thrown in to make her feel that she'd at least had a 'proper hot meal'. Her drinking had also stepped up a notch. She no longer felt the same emotional numbing as she had done. She now found herself spending her whole day going to buy alcohol, drinking it and recovering from its effects. But there was now something else. On a morning that was just like any other, she woke up in blind panic, her heart racing like the clappers, drenched in sweat and with a sickly feeling in her stomach. She reached for the bottle and found immediate relief. A cycle that perpetuated, with the first drink of the day now being on waking. Peggy started asking Pat to do her shopping for her, although Pat discovered that she had to throw out food that was out of date. Babs was asked by Peggy to collect the prescription for her blood pressure tablets and take it to the chemist. The tell-tale signs were there. Babs and Pat sensed that something was not right. It was Pat who had noticed Peggy's slurred speech on the telephone and first thought that Peggy had suffered a stroke. She was about to call an ambulance, but Peggy refused and later appeared to be none the worse for wear. There was nothing obvious to give away Peggy's drinking. That is until she stumbled on the bottles of gin in a cupboard that she'd opened in error.

On a Sunday morning in early August, it was time for Pat to voice her concerns.

"Peggy, luv. I've seen you bin drinking more than you should've." Peggy shrugged.

"Don't be silly, Pat. You know that's not true."

"So you wouldn't say nothing if I took away your booze?"

"Don't you dare!" Peggy was defiant.

"Why are you being like this, Peggy? It's not doing you no good. If Mum could see you now…"

"Don't you bring Mum into it. That's a nasty thing to say and you know it."

"But, Peggy. Listen to me. If I don't say something, no one will…"

"Pat, stop nagging me. What I do is my problem. Why don't you just mind your own business?"

Pat covered put her face in her hands.

"Oh, Peggy. 'Ow could you. 'Ow could you say somefin' like that. It's mean, Peggy. It's not you.

"You're not Peggy any more. The Peggy I know wouldn't be sitting here, day in day out, drinking and sleeping. Drinking and sleeping. You've turned into an alcoholic, Peggy. You need to get 'elp!"

"How dare you!" Peggy tried to get up from her chair, but quickly retreated into it with a loud thump. Her legs felt like jelly.

"The only thing you know about drinking is looking after that drunk husband of yours."

There was pin-drop silence.

"That's it, Peggy. I've 'ad enough. You want 'elp, you get it from someone else. And I'm going to tell Babs. She ain't going to 'elp you neither."

In an instant, she was up, out and gone.

Peggy was nonplussed. So what if they chose not to help her. Rene would be only too pleased. After all, how could her drinking be a problem? An alcoholic was the drunk on the street corner. The Friday night binge with a kebab, vomiting into the gutter. It wasn't Peggy. It wasn't Peggy Lighterman. Besides, she still had her memory. Maybe not everything she'd done in the last few days, but she still remembered everything in the past. She knew that it was coming up to Mum's death anniversary. This was the first year that she wouldn't be able to make it to the cemetery.

With three girls to feed and clothe, Mum needed to be in paid employment. Fortunately, she wasn't far from home, working at McDougall's flour mill at Millwall Docks. As for child care, that was the boon of living in Bermondsey. Peggy had her nan living upstairs, cousins just down the road and friends who looked out for each other. All in all, she probably had more first or second cousins living within a stone's throw of her flat than she could count on her fingers and toes. At least Mum didn't have to worry about shepherding the 'terrible three' to and from school.

Peggy's family were poor by today's standards, but not living hand-to-mouth. Of course, they knew plenty of families who didn't know where their next meal was coming from. The self-righteous chattering classes would say that Bermondsey was full of petty criminals. Stealing wasn't right, but it often meant the difference between living and starving. Moralistic judgements are a different matter when you live a life of poverty. If you couldn't get a job on the docks, in the Print or in the Market, life was grim. Childhood disease was rife. Rickets, polio and bronchitis were all too common. When Babs was born, Pat's earliest memory was her mother's constant checking on her sister at night, to see if she was all right. Babies being buried on Sundays were all too common and Peggy's mum didn't want any of her children to be yet another casualty.

As if that wasn't enough, there were the rats. Scurrying here and there. Not just in the warehouses on the quays but also in people's homes. The rat catcher was a not uncommon sight in buildings along the Old Kent Road. Others would simply hawk what was purported to be rat poison like snake oil salesman. "Them rats been munchin' the floorboards again?" echoed through dark musty hallways. From London Bridge to Tower Bridge; Borough to Bankside; Walworth to Blackfriars. Children across the length and breadth of the docks told each other stories as they slept in the dark of Jack Black, the nineteenth-century rat catcher. Legend had it that he would make rats appear from his coat and 'tame them', showing the crowds how he had remained unbitten after handling a bundle of those mangy vermin. Space was at a premium. The Lightermans had three girls sharing a room and three families sharing one outside toilet. Bath time was a tin bath hanging in the kitchen, with the whole family sharing the water. God forbid the days when Cyril had to contend with a shipment of coal. The bath water was so black that the children were dirtier after than before their bath. Breakfast was bread and jam. Lunch was bacon and bread. Supper, bread and tomatoes. Sometimes eggs and cheese. Potatoes and cabbage replaced more expensive food such as beef, milk and fresh fruit. Leftovers were carried over into other meals for the week. Dripping from whatever meat was eaten substituted for butter or margarine. Hessian sack cloth for potatoes was made into Peg rugs. It was make do and mend. Any holes in clothing were darned with whatever was available.

Hand-me-downs were the norm. Peggy had seen worse. Much worse. Houses riddled with damp, leaking ceilings, rotting and sagging floor boards, soot covered walls, wonky tables and chairs propped up by folded cardboard. Children who looked permanently hungry. Families would always be looking for something to pawn for a shilling to get the brown bread, rice and potatoes that would stave off starvation. Mothers with hair uncombed. Fathers unshaven.

The Lightermans still didn't have all mod cons such as lino and wallpaper. For Mum, washing day would be a scrubbing brush and board with common soda and Sunlight soap but she was fortunate enough to have a mangle. By the end of the day, her red raw hands would be sore and aching. The hands that had carried her children and emptied sacks of wheat at the flour mill were the hands of hope that were wrapped around her family to keep them from the ravages of poverty and disease. If they were desperate to keep their heads above the breadline, some fathers would resort to boxing to supplement their non-existent earnings. Fathers fought to feed their families. If you walked down the Old Kent Road, you'd see a boxing club in nearly every block of buildings – the

Thomas A Becket being the most prestigious around that area, where boxing legend Joe Rolfe was often seen training.

Closer to the docks was the Fisher Downside Club, originally for young Catholic boys to get some exercise and learn some discipline. Cyril used to talk about 'Ernie down the docks…part-time docker, part time boxer'. 'Box for a pound' signs were seen on pub doors, which is where many fights took place when Cyril was a young man. London Prizing Rules meant all was above board. No free for all but three-minute rounds with gloves and referees. Mum once went in search of Cyril at the Eight Bells Pub in Bermondsey Street and told the girls that she had seen a picture of Tom Causer. She'd also seen similar legends at *The Ring* in Blackfriars. Dockers would watch the fight drinking what Cyril would call 'proper stock ale, with a shillin' on yer glass'. Mum would catch sight of him staggering out of one of his many locals on a Saturday night, the place buzzing with horses and carts, traps and ponies. Boxing was in Bermondsey's blood, largely springing out of poverty to earn money. There were national champions such as Jim Sullivan and Tommy McGovern; as well as a regional ones such Phil Lundgren, Billy Tarrant, Pat O'Grady and Jonny Ould.

It seemed that for Bermondsey, pubs and boxing were inextricably bound. But with two working parents and a dad who earned over three times the average wage, at least they could afford decent living conditions and better food. That wasn't to say that Cyril didn't have vices other than drink. He would also bet on the greyhounds. Sometimes he would get lucky.

Peggy had never seen a happier Dad when he came home beaming at winning on Islandeady at the Gold Collar Cup at

Catford in 1950. But whatever had happened to Dad and his drinking, they owed him some debt of gratitude.

Day after day after day, Peggy would repeat the same cycle. Wake, drink, sleep, drink, sleep. Alcohol replaced food and just about everything else in her life. Rene and Michael had started to take on more 'errands' for Peggy. Sometimes buying tea, bread and milk, but mostly buying gin. They would also draw money out of the bank with Peggy's permission. Then when Peggy had come down with a cold one day and hadn't had a drink for the whole day, sweat pouring off her and shaking uncontrollably, she had a fit but it wasn't witnessed.

Peggy spent the whole night drowsy and as soon as she woke up, she started drinking again. She didn't know what had happened. Her body felt sore. She could see blood around her mouth when she looked in the mirror and her tongue was painful and swollen. Her nightdress smelt of wee. She realised that she must have had a fit.

Dr Hither visited again the following week. Peggy took longer to answer the door. She was still wearing her nightdress at eleven o'clock in the morning. Her demeanour had changed and there was a stale smell in her flat. The neat dyed blonde bob was now a shower of matted grey hair. Dirty plates and bowls were everywhere. Next to the bed, on the sideboard and stacked up near the sink.

"Peggy, I'm concerned about you. You don't look like you have changed your clothes for some time."

"Thanks for your concern, Doctor, but I'm just having a lie in. I often do these days. There's nothing much to do for a widow like me, is there?"

"You look as if you've lost weight since I last visited."

"Maybe a little, Doctor, but I eat what I need to."

"Can I have a quick look in the kitchen?"

Peggy was never happy with people 'snooping about' in her house and minding her business, but she acquiesced. She didn't want Dr Hither thinking that she was a totally crusty curmudgeon.

Dr Hither had a quick look in Peggy's bathroom. The bath was dry as a bone. The kitchen looked as if it hadn't been cleaned since he'd last visited. He opened the 'fridge. The smell was overpowering. He didn't stop to inspect it further and returned to the lounge. He also checked the packet containing Peggy's antidepressants, which hadn't been touched since his last visit. This time, Peggy needed more persuasion to come back into hospital.

This time Dr Hither wanted to make sure that there wasn't something that he was missing. This time, there was no Pat or Babs to accompany her to Ada Salter Ward. While they were waiting for the ambulance, Dr Salter casually asked Peggy, not thinking about it with any degree of clinical suspicion.

"I forgot to ask you, Peggy. Have you ever had a drink since Jim died? I only ask because some people often find that it helps to relax them when they feel anxious or low."

After all this time, it was the question that Peggy was least expecting but immediately, her defences were up.

"Maybe a couple of times, as nightcap."

"And how much would that be?"

"Only a pinch of gin." The distance between her thumb and third finger was barely visible.

"Where do you usually keep your alcohol?"

Peggy pointed to the cabinet at the end of her living room. It creaked loudly as Dr Hither pulled the handle. Inside was a bottle of gin, half empty.

"How long does a bottle like this last you, Peggy?"

"Maybe two days, maybe three."

Dr Hither's mind whirred as he calculated how much Peggy was drinking on average per week. It was a large amount. An amount that would put her health at huge risk and explained how he had misinterpreted her symptoms of alcohol dependence for depression. He wouldn't have been the first doctor to have overlooked alcohol as a cause of Peggy's presentation and he certainly wouldn't be the last. After all, it would be lower down on most people's list, doctor or not, to think that an older woman would be drinking heavily.

The chance discovery of Peggy's alcoholism had put a different complexion on things, but the problem wasn't just going to be if Peggy was prepared to accept that she had a problem. It would be whether she was prepared to change her drinking habits. Dr Hither knew that the journey that Peggy was on was going to be a long one. But with his help, he hoped that it would be a voyage of discovery, even though into unchartered waters. Only time would tell.

Chapter 6

The Awakening

The formalities were over. Seen by the doctor, vital signs checked by the nurse and medication prescribed. All within the space of two hours. She still couldn't get used to patients not being in bed or in their nightclothes during the day. Even for Peggy, it was the first time that she had been out of her own nightclothes for weeks. She hadn't had a drink since the afternoon and was beginning to feel a little queasy. There was a strange churning, rising from the pit of her stomach. She felt her hand trembling and her palms were moist. An inner sense of restlessness began to take over. Were these the feelings of alcohol withdrawal? She had felt the same, if not worse, that day she had come down with a cold.

"Nurse!"

She pulled herself out of the chair, holding to the wall as she walked down the corridor.

"Nurse, I've come over all funny."

Beads of sweat covered her face. A nurse came over to her, wearing a badge with 'My name is Ade' in large print. He could immediately sense that something was wrong and paged the doctor on call. Psychiatrists are trained to put patients at ease, and this is exactly what Dr Gupta did. Peggy felt reassured that she was being taken seriously.

It didn't take long for a perusal of the notes to reveal the 'possible recent alcohol misuse'. She hadn't been altogether honest with the admitting doctor.

"I'm going to prescribe you some medication for an alcohol detox, Mrs Lighterman. It will help you to feel calmer and reduce the feelings that you're experiencing. We will start with the maximum dose and gradually reduce this over the next week. We also need to give you some vitamin injections to top up a vitamin called thiamine, which is often very low in people who have problems with their diet when drinking alcohol."

Peggy had always found it funny when she heard youngsters talking about taking a 'chill pill'. Now she knew what that meant. Within an hour of taking the 'benzos' as she called them, she felt herself relax. It was as if she had taken another G and T and a double one at that! She still felt miserable. Not like before when she felt better almost as soon as had she stepped onto the ward. Her head felt heavy first thing in the morning, like a black cloud had swallowed her. She would wake up early, unable to get back to sleep and lie there, feeling as if she wouldn't mind going to sleep and not waking up. The nurses were very understanding and took great pains to ensure that she was getting plenty of fluids, even if her appetite was shot to pieces. She was asked about her energy many times. Energy. What energy? She felt exhausted even after walking to the toilet. She felt like a hollow shell. Like she did after Jim died.

What had she come to? She remembered her father. Was she slowly turning into him? She used to think that she was above it. A pitiful sight now, no longer capable of even the most rudimentary task. How had the mighty fallen.

The next day was Dr Hither's ward round. Not what she was expecting. Instead of the peripatetic entourage, it was a stationary affair, with people of all professions seated in a semi-circle around the room. All to see her 'perform'. A daunting prospect to say the least. She couldn't remember all their names, but there was Dr Hither and two other doctors. She had previously referred to them as Dr Hither's next of kin, but this met with some degree of mirth when she had spoken to one of the nurses. Junior doctors. That was it, junior doctors. Then, there was the ward manager. What happened to the term 'Matron'? Ward manager sounded like a department store. Was the NHS now a business? Next, the psychologist. Wasn't that the same as a psychiatrist? No one had bothered to explain. Lastly, there was Occupational Therapist. A group of younger people sat in the corner and were introduced as medical students and nursing students. All eyes were now on her.

"Mrs Lighterman, I am sorry that you had to come into hospital again. I know that things haven't been easy for you."

Peggy was clearly fazed by the experience. Without thinking, she launched into a monologue, but one that was tempered by a profound slowing of speech and gesture.

"I don't deserve to be here, Doctor. I've brought this on myself. Can't you see that? There are plenty of others who need my hospital bed more than I do. How you can sit there and tell me that I have depression? I don't have depression, Doctor. I've just become lazy. Very lazy. I've become just like my…like my dad. A miserable old alcoholic with no concern for anyone else but my…myself."

The room was cloaked in a hushed eerie silence.

"You know that, Doctor, don't you?" Tears rolled down Peggy's cheek like meandering rivulets of sorrow. "There's nothing you can do to get me better. I'm being punished. Punished for being such a bad person. I feel rotten inside. Rotten to the core."

With that, Peggy got up slowly, choking back the tears. She pushed her chair back, turned back around and made her way to the door. One of nurses opened the door for her, carrying some tissues and accompanied her out. Dr Hither spoke to the nurses and his junior doctors in more detail about Peggy's state of mind. There wasn't anything physical to account for her presentation. An increase in the dose of her antidepressant was made and an increased level of observation in view of what the doctors had called 'severe depressive disorder'.

Pat and Babs didn't visit Peggy, temporarily scarred by her acerbic verbal attack on Pat. But when they called the ward for an update, they could not leave her to suffer and visited her together.

They were shocked at the Peggy who appeared in front of them. She would avoid eye contact, talk in a low volume voice and would say very little. All they could do was sit with her. And they did. Often for hours with nothing said. They knew that Peggy must be ill, as it took a lot for her not to crack a joke. Their big sister was vanishing before their eyes.

With a concerted approach involving the whole ward team, two dedicated sisters, medication to treat her depression and ward-based activities to encourage social interaction, in time, Peggy was lifted from the darkness of her mind. What a wonderful profession is psychiatry, to combine expertise in healing the body and mind. Pat and Babs couldn't praise the staff enough. First, Peggy's appetite started to improve, and she was taken off food supplements. Then her sleep got better. No longer waking early and feeling unrefreshed. Some days later, the feeling of being weighed down by extreme tiredness was also slowly disappearing.

She felt for the patients on the ward. Mental illness is a terrible thing to have and being away from your home and loved ones must be equally upsetting. Peggy would be a casual onlooker at mealtimes, gazing around trying to guess what might be wrong with each patient. She knew some of their names through the nurses speaking to them or simply because she had talked or had tried to talk to them.

Ted was an imposing man who was always dressed brightly; his cheerfulness infectious. He couldn't keep still at mealtimes, striding around the dining room, talking loudly, laughing, making jokes and being a little overfamiliar with the ladies. He would sometimes come and sit next to Peggy, talking incessantly, moving from topic to topic at a rate of knots, with tenuous connections between them.

"All right, luv. I'm Ted. Enough said. Lying in bed. Do you like your dinner? It's dinner time, followed by telly. I like telly, not jelly. The soaps. Carbolic soap on a rope. It gets me clean. No point in being dirty, Gertie. Gertie from down the road. Jamaica Road. Jamaica? No, she went of her own accord…"

Peggy knew that she was getting better when she often found herself on the verge of laughing when she saw him talking to others, but she never did. That would be cruel. He couldn't help it, poor soul. Did he have bipolar? Although he was entertaining with his use of words, he was also clearly not well. She knew that, were he to see himself like this when he was better, it would no doubt upset and embarrass him. She would never forget the way he always ended his conversation-well, usually a one-sided monologue with the doctor. "Be lucky, Doc. Be lucky!"

Audrey was a small, delicate looking lady who always wore the same gold necklace. Petite and bespectacled with a voice as sweet as Babycham, that would melt your heart, she leaned to one side and used a frame to walk, usually supported by a nurse on each side to steady her gait. Even with a hearing aid in each ear, she would still be barely able to make out what the nurses were saying to her. She would answer each question with "Yes, nicely, thank you, dear." Except when she was being changed! She occupied the room next to Peggy. On one occasion when the nurses were giving her what Peggy called a 'wash and brush up', she could hear one of the nurses speak in a calm and reassuring voice. "Audrey, we need to change you. You've had a bit of an accident with your water works. Is that all right?" There was no answer. "Audrey, I just need to help you get changed. I am one of the nurses. I'm Larry."

After a pregnant pause, came the response, loud and clear, "Don't be so silly, of course I'm not married and I'm not about to be. Now get off me…"

It can't be easy having to tend to someone who has been moved from their home to an unfamiliar environment, not appreciating the extent of their dementia and having someone to wash and dress them. Peggy was full of admiration for them. Changing people who were heavily soiled but resistive to any attempts to ensure their cleanliness and dignity. You had to give them time, explain each step of what you were going to do, be calm, always, and sometimes just come back after a few minutes. Dementia was like that. No two days would be the same. The doctors would see the patients for, at most, half an hour at a time. For nurses, it was considerably longer. For carers, it was permanent. There were some patients who, like Peggy, were there because they were feeling out of sorts. Peggy couldn't put it any other way. She'd had it explained to her so many times. Her GP, Dr Hither, the other doctors, the nurses. Even what she'd seen on the telly in the soaps. It was a chemical imbalance, a stress reaction, something in your childhood, something in your genes. Looking at the papers, it could even be something in your tea! But Peggy had still yet to consider something else. The effect of her drinking.

Six weeks into her admission. Pat and Babs were sitting quietly, both reading. Peggy piped up. "What lies trembling at the bottom of the ocean?"

Pat disconnected momentarily from that day's newspaper.

"What's that, Peggy luv?"

"I said what lies trembling at the bottom of the ocean?"

Pat was taken aback. She looked over to an equally astounded Babs.

"I dunno, Peggy, what?"

"A nervous wreck, Pat. A nervous wreck."

It didn't take long to light the fuse of incandescence like the blue touch paper on a firework. The three sisters were doubled up, each crying their own tears of sorrow and joy. It was a unique synchrony of emotion that had united them once again.

"She's back, Babs. Our Peggy is back!"

It was a day the terrible three would never forget. An indelible imprint on their hearts and minds. Again, at peace. With themselves and one another.

Towards the middle of her admission, Dr Hither had asked Peggy at the ward round if it would be all right to test her memory, just to check and see if there were any problems. Peggy didn't know that drinking could affect someone's memory. Later the same morning, the ward doctor came to see her in her room to carry out some memory tests. Peggy was watching the news. She always liked to be well informed.

The headline 'new nasal spray for dieting' scrolled across the screen. Peggy shrugged her shoulders. There's a war in Iraq, she reflected, and they're talking about drugs for dieting. People were going hungry in the world. Times had changed. Children these days would rather spend time on playing video games than out playing with their friends. A strange world indeed. Dr Gupta was dressed like anyone else would be who was going to the office but Peggy noticed that he wasn't wearing a stethoscope around his neck and not accompanied by a gaggle of others. Just Dr Gupta, a pleasant disposition and a thin file containing an assortment of questions that would no doubt, by the end of proceedings, challenge and confound her.

"Peggy, I'm just to going to ask you some questions about your memory and other things. I know that they might seem too easy for you, but I ask everyone the same questions. Is that all right with you?"

"I'm not daft, Doctor. I've still got all my faculties intact, but I'll do the best I can." Peggy awaited the starter for ten.

"Can you tell me the year?"

"2003, Doctor."

"The month?"

"Erm, November?"

"The day?"

"Monday. Is that correct, Doctor?"

"It's actually Tuesday."

Peggy was a day out but thought that it must it be easy to lose track being in hospital.

"…and the date?"

"We must be somewhere near the beginning…the beginning of the month. The 10th?"

Dr Gupta didn't correct Peggy, but it was the 18th.

"Where are we now, Peggy? What's this place called?"

Peggy rattled off not just the ward and floor, but the country, county, city, her full address and postcode.

"Now that's just silly. What silly questions!" Peggy was starting to feel a little patronised.

"The next few questions are not so easy, but just do your best." Dr Gupta continued the set piece.

"I'm going to give you three words to remember and I'm going to ask you to repeat them to me so that I know that you have heard them correctly and then ask you again in a few minutes.

"Carpet, ruler, bottle." He made sure that he left enough time between each word to allow Peggy to commit them to memory.

"Carpet, ruler, bottle." Peggy's full concentration was commanded.

Dr Gupta then went through a series of other questions and tasks, including repeating words, naming objects, carrying out a set of instructions, recalling the three objects, reading, writing and copying shapes.

"Thank you, Peggy." He peered down at his score sheet and began totting up the scribbled numbers.

"What's the score, Doctor, if you'll pardon the pun, Doctor?"

"The score is out of 30 and you scored 27."

What Peggy didn't know was that for her level of ability, dropping point for not knowing the day and date, recalling only 2 out of the 3 words and having problems copying the shapes, the score meant that she was showing problems that were not normal. Peggy looked perturbed.

"It is Alzheimer's, Doctor?"

Dr Gupta leaned in. "It doesn't look like it's Alzheimer's, Peggy. It's probably more likely to be the early signs of damage to your brain from alcohol." He went on to ask her what she thought were questions that couldn't possibly be answered by anyone but the winner of Mastermind.

"The part of the brain most affected by alcohol does not cause problems with memory, but with things like planning ahead and finding solutions to problems that we might call thinking outside the box."

Peggy had noticed that, even though she had started to feel brighter in mood, she now found it difficult to hold more than one piece of information in her head at once and was generally slower at taking in what people said to her.

Dr Gupta went on to explain that, at this stage, stopping drinking completely would almost certainly stop any further damage in its tracks and that there may even be the possibility that her memory would start to improve as the parts of the brain damaged by alcohol would start to repair. He also suggested a scan of her head, which meant her lying in what looked like a small, white tunnel for half an hour. The scan came back not showing any evidence of any changes to the structure of her brain. Dr Gupta even showed her the brain scan, which looked to Peggy just like a giant cauliflower.

Over the following weeks, Peggy was allocated a community nurse, Mary, who came to visit Peggy on the ward. The process of what the ward referred to as 'discharge planning' had started. Peggy had entered a bottomless pit and had climbed out bruised and battle-scarred. But she was still in one piece but one that was just that bit more fragile. As she bade farewell to Ada Salter Ward, Pat's 'old banger' as she called it, was waiting in the visitor's car park and a safe journey home was negotiated into the late summer dusk of their beloved Bermondsey.

Dr Hither spotted Peggy outside from his office, with one of the nurses assisting Pat in fitting Peggy's assortment of bags and baggage into the boot of the car.

It wasn't Peggy's depression and alcoholism that had struck a chord with him, it was her vulnerability. A vulnerability that he knew only too well.

Theo Hither had what you might call an unusual childhood for a future doctor. Although his parents were middle class professionals, money didn't follow their profession as teachers. They had a stark choice. A bigger house in a leafy neighbourhood or a smaller one around a council estate. The latter would mean spending their earnings on a Private School education. In the best interest of their two children, they chose the latter. Yet, the traditional school to which Theo and his older brother Adam were sent was perhaps not the most inclusive one. To be fair, nor were many others. Theo was at infant school when Adam had joined King Edward the Martyr school.

What they didn't realise at the time was that Adam's experiences would be life-changing for both himself and for Theo. One month into the first term, Theo had returned from school one day to hear his father on the telephone to Adam's school. On placing down the receiver, he overheard his parents.

"That was the school. They want to us to come in first thing tomorrow to see Miss Peters." He thought it unusual to be summoned in such a manner, particularly for a child still in the formative years of their voyage into mastering the intricacies of social skills. "But Adam excels at everything. He always has."

Jonathan pondered on the sudden interest in his son's welfare, but they took time off work nonetheless and made the appointment in good time. It transpired that Adam had filled one of the other boy's pockets with sand, for no reason that anyone could fathom. Both parents and head teacher agreed that this was probably a one-off, but the school would need to be vigilant about any further incidents. But there would be more. Many more. On another occasion, Theo's father would have to plead with the head not to expel his son for touching the head of a commuter on the train to school. When asked why he did this, he replied "I just wanted to find out what it felt like." It may not have come as a surprise to Jill and Jonathan that Adam was behaving oddly. Jill had always considered Adam to be a bit eccentric, but this had merged into something altogether different. In the summer holidays before starting at St Edward's as it was known, some of the mums had said Adam had been rude to their children. Not just the "you smell" or "I'm not your friend" sort of rudeness parents might hear. Adam had started making rude comments to his friends. They were personal comments that were hurtful, such as telling his best friend, having got his legs stuck in the swing, that he was a "fatso" and proceeded to walk away instead of offering help. The popular, happy-go-lucky boy who had boasted about inviting more people to his seventh birthday party than anyone else, had become a boy that no one wanted to know.

Perhaps his parents saw it coming but lived in denial. After two years, when Theo joined the same school, the first day was one like no other.

"You! Are you Hither's brother?" was the first 'greeting' from a much older boy.

Surnames were the usual epithet at such a school. Theo nodded, expecting some preliminary camaraderie.

"Your brother's queer." It didn't mean what it does now. In the 1970s, it meant 'odd'.

With each step, came muffled whispers.

"Look, Hither's brother."

"Is he queer too?"

"He's probably the same."

Starting in a different school is every child's worst nightmare. For Theo, the relentless onslaught continued from all corners of the school. In fact, Theo quickly resorted to bribing sixth formers to protect him from potential bullies with sweets using money that he stole from his mother. Otherwise, life would have been even more unbearable. Theo was eventually able to integrate and integrate well, once his peers had sized him up as being "nothing like your brother." Year after year and year, Theo would watch helplessly as his brother was bullied daily. Much of it was provoked by inappropriate comments from Adam to boys he could ill afford to tease. The cruelty was relentless.

A particularly callous practice was for boys with whom Adam shared a daytime study room to make Adam crouch under the table, which they would surround with towels and boil a kettle next to it so that steam passed through it under the table and made him gasp for air. Adam was kept there forcibly until he agreed to rehearse and recite disgusting and depraved rhymes. On another occasion, Theo remembered as if it were yesterday the time when he saw a much bigger boy "boxing" with Adam. By boxing, this meant punching the hell out of him. Theo joined his brother in brotherly opposition to quell the heavy blows, but the relentless onslaught of punches was too much, and Theo eventually had to back off.

Adam was remarkably vulnerable but the supposedly respected and well-established school did nothing to make his life more bearable. They were probably aware, but such schools had either the attitude that it was character building or else victims of bullying, harassment or intimidation were told to "turn the other cheek." Less than helpful attitudes in the scheme of things for a child's psychological development. Every time he watched an episode of *Tom Brown's Schooldays*, Theo's skin would crawl. At King Edward's, there wasn't just one Flashman, but an endless supply. Adam was academically gifted. At the age of nine, his ability to recite every single football result in League Division One for that season was second to none.

It flew in face of reason that this was the same boy who couldn't generate even the most rudimentary social overture. The family had high hopes when he went into the Sixth Form of a different and much more accepting school, but he started having problems concentrating. Theo's parents were at a loss to explain why. After getting into a Polytechnic to study accountancy, his life became an endless stream of major life difficulties.

By this time, Theo was in medical school, while Adam left his higher studies with no qualifications after he had failed his end of year exams at the Polytechnic. What followed was a downward spiral of life events. He was sacked from a series of jobs. The first was at an accountancy firm, where he spent all day just staring out of the window. He then worked as a porter at the local hospital but was eventually asked to leave when witnessed by visitors lying in the middle of the corridor. The family were desperate for an answer. Influenced heavily by his experience of Adam's problems, Theo suggested that the family see a psychiatrist. Finally, there was some closure for the family. Adam was referred to a doctor specialising in what were called developmental disorders and diagnosed with Asperger's Syndrome. This explained his problems with social interaction, being unable to read the body language of others and not being able interact in a socially acceptable manner. The diagnosis was an answer but there was no treatment as such. They tried family therapy, but Father would often not attend. He hadn't yet come to terms with how this could have happened to his brilliantly gifted son. But the story didn't end there. Adam's behaviour became more and more bizarre. Now in his early 30s, still unable to hold down a job, he continued to live with his parents. Not only that, he started to become more irritable and increasingly suspicious of others. Several years passed. Adam had started withdrawing into himself. Spending more time in his room, often in bed or just walking around the area aimlessly. When Theo met him,

Adam would talk very little but often make strange expressions and laughed for no reason.

Then, one day, his parents called their GP to say that Adam was talking about feeling so miserable that he was thinking of taking his life. But the strangest turn of events was yet to come. It was a total coincidence that Theo was a junior doctor at the same hospital to which Adam was admitted on that humid July evening and just happened to be the on-call junior doctor. He couldn't do it. He just couldn't bring himself to admit his own brother to hospital. Lucky for Theo that another doctor happened to be around. Adam's admission lasted some months and Theo would often see Adam when he was on call, either on the same ward that he was seeing another patient or simply walking around the grounds.

Adam's psychiatrist changed the diagnosis from Asperger's to schizophrenia. Theo wasn't sure about how a developmental disorder could have metamorphosed into a serious mental illness but acquiesced against his better judgement. After all, Adam didn't hear voices. Or did he? His psychiatrist seemed to think so. Families are so often in denial. Maybe Theo chose to ignore the repetitive idiosyncratic speech, distractibility and muttering to himself, or maybe to voices, that Adam had displayed over the past few years. No one, certainly not Theo or his family, could have predicted what would happen from then onwards. After starting treatment for schizophrenia, Adam had never looked back. Although he progressed through a series of hostels and half-way houses, at the age of 38, he finally started living independently. Although not having secured paid employment since then, he had remained as well as he could be. Adam was a sensitive and vulnerable child who grew into an angry and frightened adult. In a way, psychiatry had saved him. He was now more socially responsible and emotionally aware as he had ever been. A miracle, Theo thought, that a mental illness such as this could have ravaged someone's life for so long, robbing them of their childhood and much of their adulthood, and then be treated with few complications. The lifelong experience of mental illness had made Theo into a different person than he might otherwise have been. Probably more caring and certainly a fierce advocate for the hidden and marginalised. He could turn his training as both doctor and psychiatrist into offering the best possible treatment for a group of vulnerable older people whom society had overlooked and cast aside. The forgotten population of alcoholics. The world had thrown up its hand and offered one large firm shrug to Peggy. It was up to Theo to catch her if she fell back into the chasm of hopelessness and despair that had silently smothered her senses and deprived her of a life worth living. He would not stop fighting for change. For delivering care that people needed. People in Bermondsey didn't ask for much, but that didn't mean they didn't deserve the best. The very best. He looked again at his watch. It was time to go home, but it was also a unique time for Dr Hither. It was time to change the world. Not with a closed fist, but with an open hand.

Chapter 7
Best Foot Forward

Peggy still lived with her mum when she got married to Jim. Both wanted to be sure about their betrothal and be financially secure before they set up home as one. They got engaged four years previously and were ready to tie the knot. It was December 1962 and just when they were thinking of setting a wedding date, Cyril died following an attack of alcoholic hepatitis and then liver failure. Peggy was devastated. A piece of her had gone forever. Whatever her dad had been like, he had provided well and was always proud of her. She would never forget that. When she returned from St Saviour's Hospital with her mum and sisters on that frosty Christmas morning, their breath like a cloud of cold steam silhouetted against the shower of bright yellow beams raining down into the hospital car park, she felt a hollowness that she thought would never go away. But Peggy and Jim's love for each other was strong and an insurmountable force pulled them more strongly. They finally tied the knot in the Spring of '64, with Peggy aged 31 and Jim 36. With The Beatles' *Can't Buy Me Love* at Number 1, they were on cloud nine. A marriage almost certainly made in heaven. Peggy's mum had no hesitation in welcoming Jim to the Lighterman fold. His unprepossessing aspirations made a goodness of fit that eased his passage into family life, to tarry in her humble abode until they were ready to move on. Jim left the docks with a meagre pension, as this scheme had only started some nine years previously, but there was work at St Saviour's Hospital and he found his feet again.

The working life of a porter bore a striking resemblance to that of the docking fraternity. The workforce was mainly men and, like it or not, their banter may not have been politically correct, but it's what got them through the day. A culture that remains to this day and will probably never change. The difference was the working conditions. The Porters' Lodge at St Saviour's was spacious and had a separate common room with a TV. It was warm, with a place to sit and eat. A stark contrast to sitting on the filthy floor of the wharf or dockside steps come sun, rain or snow. Shifts were predictable, sometimes day, sometimes night, with time off in-between. It was far from humdrum, but the legwork was back breaking. On hot summer days, by the end of the shift, Jim bore the appearance of long-distance runner, pouring with sweat as he wheeled heavy gas canisters along meandering basement corridors. If only Canada dock had fitted showers, the weary worker would not have to inflict the consequences of a hard day's night on the unsuspecting users of public transport. Morning shifts would start at seven, sharp. The first day is always the most memorable with any change of circumstances. After a quick brew and a digestive quickly interrupted by the crackling of the walkie talkie. Jim reached for the radio to turn it down, but it went flying across the room, rolling over several times, before it landed, still in one piece, on top of a copy of a popular tabloid, the headline reading “A week is a long time in politics.” With this start, Jim thought he’d be lucky if he managed a week in this job. The toe tapping chords of *Bad Moon Rising* continued to echo across the room, continuing to belt out its staccato rhythm.

“Patient for X-Ray. Patience Ward. Repeat Patience Ward.” The voice fell silent. Jim salvaged the offending article and clicked it off.

“Patient for X-Ray. Patience Ward. Repeat Patience Ward. Please respond.”

“Got that, Ted.” There was no mistaking the voice. “Be over there soon mate.” Jim pulled out a wheelchair, each one standing in an orderly fashion like passengers queuing on a taxi rank. His hands and arms bore the stigmata of his docking past, scarred and rough like worn out sandpaper.

We seem comfortable talking to people we know are willing to listen but also those who do not judge us. Even more so if we know that we are unlikely to see them again. It could be the hairdresser, the commuter or the porter. Betty was keen to talk. She had fallen over while staying with her daughter whilst over from Kent. It was a nasty fall, but surprisingly, nothing broken. They just wanted to check out her brainbox, as she called it, to see “if there’s anything in that space between me ears.” Jim always erred on the side of caution when showing an emotional reaction. It was only polite. He responded as well as he could without being unreceptive. “Yeah, just as well to get it checked out, luv.”

It was non-stop. Moving gas cylinders, sharps bins, patients. Anything and everything. Most scary of all was moving dead bodies to and from the mortuary. Jim was no stranger to death. That dockworker who happened to be standing in the wrong place at the wrong time when the crane discharged its containers in the main hold could easily curtail a man's life just like that. Accidents, loss of limbs, concussion. He'd worn the T-shirt. But not moving dead bodies. The most rewarding part of the job was patient contact. Coming face-to-face with people in all manner of states and adding that extra something to making their day that bit easier was immensely satisfying. The acutely ill older person. The frightened child and their carer. The angry, the upset, the agitated. Not to mention the comedian, the showman and other patients putting the world to rights.

When he'd get home, his legs aching like billy-o, it was straight to Cyril's armchair to put his feet up with a copy of the local rag and the TV blaring in the background. Peggy's mum would have supper steaming on the hob. Nothing fancy, usually bangers and mash, steak and kidney pie, toad in the hole or bubble and squeak. None of this posh rubbish as Peggy's mum so eloquently put it. Just good old-fashioned honest British grub. Always tasty and washed down with a ginger ale. If they were lucky, there might be jam roly-poly for afters. Peggy would be back from school an hour before Jim. Her approach to education was never eroded during all the years served at Paradise Street Primary, her old school. She mixed kindness with discipline and would always go the extra mile if little Billy or little Johnny were struggling. But Peggy didn't suffer fools gladly, so woe betide any child chattering or looking out of the window. But no chalk throwing. No caning. Not even a smack. Just a stern glare. The sort that a certain bear from popular children's story would often deliver. She was popular and previous children would often great her in the street, with "Good afternoon,

Miss Lighterman." By the time Peggy had served her time, some even had children of their own going to the same school.

In 1966, it was time to move on. Jim had hired a van to move their belongings from the Bellamy to their new flat on the Chuzzlewit estate. Still all concrete, but this time more of it spread over a larger area. They'd all come to help. Pat, Babs, their husbands and children. Neighbours also lent a hand. It was the spirit of Bermondsey. The Bellamy Estate was testament to the new land of concrete that had started to dominate south London. Peggy and Jim lived there for nearly twenty-five years before it was earmarked for demolition. It was a period of huge social upheaval. Perhaps the biggest change was the aftermath of their beloved Bermondsey merging with the borough of Southwark. To outsiders, it heralded a new era which saw the end of right to tenancy based on having a family connection with the borough. To Peggy and Jim, it was a final act of treason, a constant theme repeated and again that Dr Hither was later to hear wedged into every patient consultation. Bermondsey would never be the same again. Bombing during the War, the closure of an industrial heartland, a loss of community spirit and the word that every resident dreaded hearing.

The catastrophic death knell of change. The word was regeneration.

Back on her settee, Peggy felt alive again. Rejuvenated by the treatment she'd received, she felt more prepared to continue life's journey than she had been for some months. This time, she'd agreed to something new. Something that she had never heard of before. Dr Hither called it a 'care package'. Having a carer come into her home was a novel experience for Peggy. She had always been fiercely independent, always in charge of the situation. Someone coming in and minding her business was not initially well received, but she couldn't keep relying on her sisters.

The carer arrived at seven thirty in the morning, the day after Peggy's discharge from Ada Salter Ward. She did think about not answering the door, but a very large thought bubble considered that this would be more trouble than it was worth.

"Good morning, Peggy, I am Bola." A petite uniformed lady with an exuberance and smile that would engage even the most unwilling of people in need, greeted her.

Peggy reciprocated with the somewhat more subdued response of "Hello, dear. I suppose you'd better come in."

The carer put down her somewhat overfilled handbag by the front door and carefully extracted a blue folder, whose contents were to contain the written records of all her comings and goings and what was done in-between.

"Let me just look, Peggy. Thank you. We are going to be helping you with…err…preparing breakfast and prompting you with taking your tablets. In the evening we will be…" She cast her eye down the printed sheet, all neatly typed. "…in the evening, it is the same as the morning. Preparing your evening meal and prompting with your medication."

Now there was a term that Peggy abhorred. Medication. Why couldn't she say medicines or tablets? The teacher in her began to stir again. "Also, we are going to be helping with cleaning and shopping once a week."

In hospital, Peggy had acquiesced to this help but had been steadfast in her wish to continue doing her own laundry. How could she entrust such a skilled procedure to a total stranger? The carer looked no older than Pat's daughter and Peggy doubted if she had ever even washed her own clothes, let alone someone else's. What if her smalls shrunk by being washed at too high a temperature? What if her whites weren't washed at a high enough one? The thought of bobbles on her cardie or the colour from her dress turning her undies a lurid green didn't bear thinking about. It just wasn't done.

"I don't need all that, dear, I'm sure." Peggy's defiance was flavoured with a generous helping of politeness. "Can we try for a week or two, please, Peggy and then review it again?"

The *impasse* needed to be resolved and Peggy backed down. She was just grateful that someone wasn't going to be coming in and pulling her in all directions by trying to wash and dress her. She certainly wasn't having any of that malarkey. Finally, back to the old Peggy and there was now tomorrow. Tomorrow was the day she would get her hair done.

Olu, another carer, visited again the next morning, bright as a button and with a genuine desire to help. Peggy would give it a try, at least for a few weeks. A week later, her nurse visited. Peggy had received a letter from Dr Hither's Community Mental Health Team the day after discharge, so knew that she would be receiving another visitor. Mary, her nurse, or Community Psychiatric Nurse to be precise, had taken some time to find the block. There were many similar looking buildings, as Dr Hither had previously found himself.

"Sorry I'm late, Peggy. I'm Mary, your nurse. Can I come in?" Mary was a middle-aged lady with a pleasant demeanour and gentle approach.

"Please excuse the mess. I usually take a duster around the place." It was clear that Peggy was house-proud. Only the most diligent of inspections would have unearthed even the thinnest layer of dust. The flat was as it had been when Dr

Hither first visited. Mary noticed a large collection of dolls in the front sitting room.

"They look lovely, Peggy. Where are they from?" Each was dressed in what can only be described as traditional costume, all carefully arranged around the room. Some decorating the windowsill, others on the mantelpiece and tables.

"Oh, those. Those are from my travels with Jim. We used to go on holiday every year. Not far, mind you. Just around Europe. They were happy times. Times to remember. This one even plays a tune…"

She wound up a flamenco dancer holding a classic pose, both hands held curved about her head, dressed in a bright red dress, with tied back jet-black hair. The toreador song from Carmen jingled its music box melody. "But that's all gone now and I'm nearly over it, but still these pangs, you know. It just, well, hits you when you least expect it."

Mary looked at the pictures of Peggy and Jim on the wall. The wedding photographs. One where they were sipping cocktails overlooking the sea. Another of Jim in his Sunday best.

"I put them away in the cupboard when he first went. I couldn't bear to be reminded of…" She welled up and quickly plucked a tissue from the box. "…I'll have to cope now. I'll just have to…"

Mary sat for nearly an hour, listening actively to everything that Peggy had to say. Sometimes, she interjected sensitively, without judgement, but with acceptance, warmth, empathy and an unconditional positive regard. Peggy would frequently intersperse her narrative with "I've never told anyone that before." Mary knew that this was also difficult for patients to put their feelings into words. She also suggested the possibility of seeing a psychologist, but Peggy said that she would think about it. At the end of their session, Mary got up and walked towards the front door. Peggy put her hand on her head in embarrassment.

"I'm sorry, Mary. I should have offered you a cup of tea. I don't know what came over me. I must have just got carried away wittering on." Mary politely declined. She had two more visits that morning and time was getting on.

"That's OK, Peggy. Another time maybe. I'll make sure that your GP lets the pharmacy know to post your tablets to you. I'll see you in two weeks."

Peggy felt a palpable sense of security in what was so more than a chat. It was a bond of hope. A hope for recovery. The door shut and locked, Peggy knew what she had to do. She strode to the sideboard, pulled open the door and took whatever gin was remaining to the sink. *The demon drink disappears down the drain,* she thought. Now that's alliteration she couldn't resist making! For Peggy, her flight into health was also a double-edged sword. Many people, whom she thought were her friends, started avoiding her. Or else, they would look at the ground or at their watch when speaking to her, with the obvious message that they would rather be somewhere else. She now knew who her real friends were. Babs would fly off the handle if ever Peggy mentioned this to her, fiercely protective of her big sister, with the characteristic Babsism "Don't pay no attention to 'er, Pegs luv, she ain't all that." Babs' loyalty would occasionally result in a 'standoff' down The Blue, where she could confront one of accused with "You've go' a bleedin' nerve trea'ing Pegs like that. Go on, sling your 'ook."

But time is a great healer and Peggy remained with a circle of loyal friends who would never desert her. Some didn't ask anything about Peggy's mental health, and she didn't tell them. Others closer to her would want to know more, some of whom had experienced a breakdown before.

About three months after her discharge, Peggy was getting out and about more regularly. She also started looking after herself better. A lot better. There was always a routine when it came to her tablets. Morning one for blood pressure, stomach acid and her 'dodgy ticker' as she called it. Then there was the evening sleeping tablet. Peggy wasn't alone when it came to not completely understanding accepting her depression. Many didn't see it as a mental illness but a moral failing. You couldn't see it, not like a broken leg or a red eye. But she still called it her sleeping tablet, although her GP had said that it was for her 'nerves'. She knew that, but, to Peggy, telling people that she was on a sleeping tablet just seemed to be a better way of describing it. *It was a shame*, she thought, *if people really knew she had suffered a nervous breakdown, they would think that she was mad. It was also a shame that the way society perceived mental illness was still in the middle ages.*

There finally came a time when the carer would start finding Peggy with her breakfast or evening meal prepared and having taken her medication. It didn't take long for her to climb to the next step in her recovery. She started going out shopping by herself, without Pat or Babs by her side. First, The Blue and The Lane and then further afield to Lewisham and even to the West End. Light and heavy housework was no longer a problem and home care a distant memory. She was in rude health. Most remarkable of all, was her abstinence from alcohol, of which she could be justly proud. It wasn't long after that Mary started coming to see her less often and she was discharged from Dr Hither's team. She was lucky to have Rene. Rene had been Peggy's closest friend and confidante since their primary school days at Paradise Street Primary School. *The best days of your life. They're not wrong there,* she thought. But Peggy's darkest secret would never come out of the shadows. Her drinking.

Rene had found an earthworm on her way to school. She'd never seen one before. It looked like a little finger twisting around like a whirling dervish desperate to escape the painful burning rays of the morning sun. She towered over the helpless creature, lifting it gently into her hand. Having carried it past the school gates like a waiter finely balancing a food tray on his outstretched hand, she finally released it onto the grey tarmac of the school playground. It was Peggy's second day at school. She was a shy girl, but inquisitive, nonetheless.

As Peggy stood in the playground waiting for the bell to sound, there was a girl next to her, kneeling and watching with intense concentration something in one of the hopscotch squares on the ground in front of her. Rene stood up and turned to Peggy.

"That's my ca'erpillar, that is. Do you like it?"

"That's a worm, not a caterpillar. They don't like to be in the sun. We should cover it up." No one knew more about nature than Peggy. She was an inquisitive child.

The two girls, Rene the carrier and Peggy the guard, escorted the creature towards a tree, where they ensured its transit to darkness and a safe return to the soil. They felt justly proud of their duty to nature. After all, they had saved a life.

They held hands and skipped back to the disorderly line-up of restless, fidgety, chattering cherubs. The school bell rang, commanding a sudden silence, for the hurly burly to return within moments as the throng jostled for position around the ominous teak doors. Doors that may well have even passed through the hands of a Deal Porter in years gone by. Still holding hands tightly, the girls joined the procession, their lifelong friendship already well and truly cemented.

Peggy and Rene had often reminisced about their schooldays together. The day when they got sent out of class for talking. Or the one where Rene was spotted by one of the teachers kissing Jack from the next-door school at lunchtime. But anyone would have had a job trying to dig the dirt on Peggy. Not without her share of mischief, it would never reach the threshold for playground gossip. Peggy had been to Rene and Michael's wedding, with the offer reciprocated when it came to Peggy and Jim's big moment. Jim and Michael were Best Man for each other, Peggy and Rene Chief Bridesmaid. Peggy and Jim were also godparents to Stephen, Rene's son. Even when Peggy went to Smith's College for her teacher training and Rene to work at the custard factory, time did not fray their friendship. They lived near enough to have regular contact when Peggy and Jim lived with Peggy's mum and then on the Bellamy Estate. In fact, the flat that they chose to live in on the Chuzzlewit Estate was on the same floor as Rene and Michael.

Michael was more of a regular drinker than Jim, who, when he did drink with Jim and his friends down the Blue Lion, was more likely to have a light and bitter. Even then, it was usually "mines an 'alf" when it came to ordering rounds. But Michael didn't overdo it. He knew when to stop. Like

Peggy, his father had also died from alcoholism. There was something about Bermondsey, about the lifestyle of the dockers, which meant many a man's fate was sealed when their relationship with the bottle was more than just a casual affair.

Chapter 8
Sliding Down

In his many years of service, there wasn't much that Dr Hither hadn't heard from his patients about the life and times of Bermondsey. He had seen several hundred patients in their homes at different stages of their patient journey through mental illness. It was then not surprising that the darker side of Bermondsey would rear its head. His first taste of what was regarded by some as par for the course was overhearing his ward clerk speaking to a family member about her mutual friends and acquaintances.

"Yeah, that's a shame. Yeah. Is he out of prison yet? Ain't that the third time he's bin inside?"

If it wasn't the drink, it was the clink. It was deeply ingrained in the poverty inherited over hundreds of years. There were the usual turf wars, with feuding gangs battling for control of their patch. Whilst other parts of London had largely shaken off their reputation for criminality, Bermondsey had found it more difficult. They didn't do things by halves. Robberies weren't usually low key. Going 'equipped' as they called it meant armed robberies, with gun running a known accompaniment. But 'petty thiefin'' as Cyril had put it, flowed voluminously through the veins of its society. Dr Hither once found a copy of the hospital drug formulary in a patient's house. On casually asking as to its origin, the patient triumphantly confessed that the acquisition was made when the ward had mislaid his slippers.

"If they take my bleedin' slippers, I'm going to take somethin' of theirs." It seemed to go hand-in-hand with poverty. Those with a better education, including many of Peggy's school friends, had moved out to Sidcup and Albany Park. Many of those who remained were trapped in a relentless cycle of poverty and criminality. It didn't stop with his patients. On more than one occasion, Dr Hither beheld the sight of primary school aged children being chased down the road by shopkeepers for pilfering, the child proudly parading the bag of crisps or chocolate bar as he or she scampered off down the road. Many would have heard of someone they knew, even vaguely, who'd done time inside. In fact, Dr Hither had more than his fair share of older patients who had been charged with at least one crime in their younger days. Most had mellowed with age. Others still had a temper on them, making the treatment of their mental disorders more challenging. Short of actual physical violence, there wasn't much that Dr Hither hadn't experienced. Chased out of a sheltered housing unit after discovering a patient had put up several other friends overnight, more than a little perturbed by an unwelcome visitor and still the worse for wear from drink. He had been abused and even stalked by relatives. This was mostly because his clinical judgment had gone against their wishes, such as safeguarding a patient following concerns over financial abuse.

Or considering that they needed a care home environment in their best interest, when all else had failed to protect their independence. “You ain’t puttin’ my mum in no ’ome” was an all-too-familiar response coming from what was often a collection of five or more relatives at the ward round, all arguing between themselves. The strange irony in this was often that those relatives who lived the furthest away with the least contact often projected their own feeling of guilt, complaining vehemently that services were ‘not doing enough’. There was never a dull moment and many hair-raising ones. But despite all this, Dr Hither remained faithful to improving the lot of a population who never asked for much but were hard done by through not having the opportunity to improve their health or their living conditions compared to those more privileged and with a better start in life. There was a certain raw honesty about the older generation of Bermondsey. They didn’t care whether you drove a Bentley or a Mini, whether you had cuff links or buttons or how many research papers you had published. If you showed the same respect that you would extend to any other human being, they would be indebted to you. The greatest irony was that the poorer they were, the more selfless was their attitude to life and to others. One patient stuck in Dr Hither’s memory. Living in a council flat that had gone to rack and ruin, it was cluttered with infestation and no furniture save a bed and table, his heart oozed with generosity and compassion. “If I had two pennies, I’d always give you one, Doctor. That’s just the sort of person I am.” That had touched Dr Hither even more deeply and his dedication to improving health and wellbeing merely spurred him even more strongly. This was not a generous soul in isolation. Many others would offer to pay him for being so caring, with money that would leave them without sustenance. But all good things had to come to an end, and he hung up his boots to retire from clinical practice. For Peggy, it was just before she was discharged from his community mental health team but could not have come at a worse time.

The nights were drawing in again, the Chuzzlewit Estate a sea of yellow dots in the October twilight. Peggy was going to Bingo with Irene, Pat and Babs at the Elephant. The four ladies had always paid homage to what some would call the retro fashion of their youth. For Peggy, it was the wool twin set and pearls with tweed skirt and modest square neckline. Babs was always particular about her appearance. No longer the fashionista with Kitty Foyle dress, cupid bow lipstick design and victory roll hairdo. But the chunkier heels and raglan sleeves were testament to her glamorous past.

A cut and blow dry and a bleach at the hairdressers the day before was always a prerequisite for Bingo night. Their lipsticks reflected all tones of the pink colour spectrum. No baguette, bucket or saddle bags. No shoulder straps or buckles. No plastic water bottles or mobile phones. Just a comb, tissues, perfume and purse. Although Peggy had three bags of different shapes, sizes and colours, there was always her favourite small pink one that was reserved, not for the ladies' night out, but for when she was out with Jim. Peggy never did bring that bag out again but would carry in it her own special memories.

With a firmly established routine, Wednesday was shopping day. This time, in Pat's car. A car that you could hear a mile off. Peggy never really believed that it could have passed its MOT. A clapped out 1990s Ford Fiesta that could almost be described as white with a hint of rusty orange. To Pat, it was her third baby, lovingly washed by her husband every Sunday. An exhaust change here and wheel change there, it would be back to its chipper self. Peggy sat uncomfortably on the lumpy passenger seat. She had been used to Jim's Renault, still parked in their garage and that she'd never got around to selling. A short drive away, they combined the weekly shop with a cup of tea and a sticky bun in the supermarket café. Everyone seemed to be in a rush these days. Young mums pushing fancy buggies, under the influence of a mobile phone, perambulating without due care and attention. People clearing their throat loudly behind you at the checkout if you didn't put your shopping on the conveyor belt quickly enough. Some faces that Peggy recognised, but now mostly not. Even then, more of just a "'Ello Peggy, how are you, luv?" than a leisurely chat. Some staff at the checkout were helpful, others just downright robots, as mechanical as their bar code sensors. She still missed the personalised service that she got from the selected cut of beef and nice bit of liver from the butcher or the fresh veg from the greengrocer. It had a feeling of freshness, straight from the soil and sometimes it was so fresh, you'd even find a caterpillar or other insects on it. None of these modern vacuum-packed cut vegetables in plastic. Whatever happened to brown paper bags? The choice of groceries was also beyond belief. Not just bog-standard tea these days but all manner of flavours and brands. Not just custard creams, bourbons and digestives, but a whole aisle of biscuit varieties that would send your head spinning. Before supermarkets and with no freezers, Peggy had been used to shopping every day, keeping the meat in the larder to be cooked within the few hours, not weeks. She sounded like an old fogey when she heard herself thinking aloud about no deposit no return bottles, co-op stamps and the Pools. Everything was local. There was no high street anymore.

It was dead as a doornail. If you wanted anything in a hurry, it would be from that nice Mr Patel at the corner shop, but for double the price.

Autumn came and went and so did Winter. It was a funny old December. No snow, but more variety than an episode of *The Good Old Days*. Frost, fog, rain, you name it. Shopping on Oxford Street with Pat, Babs and Rene. Presents for the nephews and nieces and a quiet tear for the babe she never had. Mince pies, Turkey and Christmas pudding. It was all over in a flash and time to look forward to her 70th.

The sisters had been preparing for Peggy's 70th birthday party for some months. The hall was booked. It was at St Matthew's Church, where Peggy had been christened. Still standing after centuries, cutting a majestic figure that dominated the Bermondsey skyline. They still marvelled at its design, being more like a small cathedral than a church, with its basilica floor plan, pointed gothic steeples, ribbed vault, Gothic arches and stained-glass windows. The Church Hall was more modern, being brick rather than stone and had a liberating sense of light and space. The guest list was close family and friends only, or else there was a danger that the world and his wife would be there. Pat and Babs' hubbies, their children and grandchildren. That's 20 already. Then there were friends and more distant relatives on the non-Lighterman side. It became 50 very quickly.

Catering was a group effort. Someone who knew someone who knew someone else. Babs was well used to organising parties, having done this for the Coronation in 1953, as well as Silver and Golden Jubilee celebrations, the latter just two years before. There'd be cheap bubbly and beer on tap. The spread would be something old and something new. Being Bermondsey, also something borrowed and no doubt something blue. There would be twiglets, vol au vents, crisps. No nuts, in case of allergies. Then there would also be cold cuts of ham and beef, potato salad, dips, sandwiches, quiche, cheese and pineapple on sticks. Someone even promised jellied eels and liquor. For pudding, there was to be arctic roll, black forest gateaux, pineapple upside down cake and a range of home backed delicacies. Mr Patel from the corner shop even offered to make samosas.

The day had arrived. Saturday, 10 January 2004. A clear blue sky and surprisingly, no rain. Peggy's expression on entering the hall, streamers flying, raucous applause, wolf whistles and a banner as if to welcome royalty. To them, she was just that. The Queen of Bermondsey. She tried not to think about Jim, but tears of joy mixed with those of sadness as hugs and kisses were in limitless supply.

The knees up went down well with old and young like, as the Lambeth Walk and Roll Out the Barrel merged mercilessly into ballads reflecting a more modern tone and tempo.

It was more than Peggy could ever have asked for, but what was still to come would change her life forever. Clearing up what remained to be done after the celebrations, Babs and Peggy were the only two left in that echoey church hall, streamers adorning the laminated floor like stripes of red, green and yellow toothpaste.

"I don't feel too good, Pegs. I think I'm comin' down with something, luv."

Peggy cast a cursory eye over Babs. Come to think of it, her clothes did look looser and her face appeared pale, sunken and gaunt. “Are you eating enough, Babs? You don’t look at all well.” Peggy had a gut feeling that this more than just fatigue from overwork. There is always that feeling you get when someone close to you isn’t quite right and you can’t put your finger on what it is. Babs promised to see her doctor the next day and Peggy accompanied her for moral support.

The surgery had recently been modernised since Peggy had last been there with Babs when she went for a follow up appointment for a review of her depression. There were new chairs in the waiting room and the place had also been given a new lick of paint. They had even updated the magazine collection, although the completely random selection of reading material in GP waiting rooms remained a mystery to Peggy. Babs asked that Peggy sit in on the consultation. Babs told Dr Chaucer that she had feeling weak for the past month and had started to get what she called “them blindin’ ’eadaches”.

He checked her over and found that her balance was not as it should be and said that there something different about her vision. He tried to explain it as best he could, but a “pale disc at the back of eye” meant that Babs needed to have some tests. Peggy went with her to every appointment. First the blood tests, from which the GP could find very little. Then the brain scan. This was all too familiar to Peggy. Having the ‘MRI’ scan was like being stuck in a tunnel in the centre of roadworks that went on for half an hour. Then came the news. It was a Wednesday in the middle of March, just two weeks after she had seen Dr Chaucer. Peggy was doing the dishes and wiping the work surfaces in the kitchen. Thought for the

Day on the radio was about the power of prayer. The phone rang from the living room. Peggy dried her hands. It was Pat. "You'd better come over 'ere soon, Peggy love. Babs has had a fit and they've taken her to hospital."

The car journey to the hospital was spent in silent sisterly togetherness as they contemplated the unknown. At the Casualty Department, Babs was asleep on a stretcher in side-room, but they could see that her face was drooping on one side. Peggy called her name, gently. Babs stirred and tried to get up but was too weak. Peggy and Pat helped her sit up straight. The ward sister arrived and showed them to her office, where she told them the news that were hoping they never wanted to hear. The brain scan showed that Babs had a tumour that was causing pressure on her brain.

This had caused the fit and was pressing on the part of her brain that controlled her movement, causing weakness on one side of the body. She would need to move to a neurosurgery ward that day. They went to get lunch in the hospital canteen and returned at visiting time. Babs remained drowsy but was more lucid come late afternoon. She apologised for causing them much "aggro" as she put it, which only made them feel even more upset. As Peggy sat watching the evening news, she could not stem the flow of tears streaming down her face. Her baby sister. How could she have let this happen? She should have done something earlier. What a big sister she turned out to be.

Then it happened. She went to Rene's flat to share her grief. Without thinking, Rene asked her what she could do. "I could do with a stiff drink" was her reply. Peggy was staring down the precipice of denial. A double G and T had sealed her future and the beginning of a slippery slope. But Peggy was blind to her future, all consumed by the overwhelming suffering of her sister. Hopeless and helpless, it was the only way of escaping a grim reality where killing the emotional pain overshadowed any contemplation of where drinking had previously carried her. Seeing her sister vanish into skin and bones before her very eyes was more than Peggy could bear. Babs remained in hospital, but she continued to go downhill both physically and mentally.

There were times when Babs would be totally lucid, but her speech remained slurred, but others when she flitted in and out of stupor. The doctors did all that they could, starting medicines that reduced the swelling in her brain. They took a sample of brain tissue, which confirmed that it was the very worst type of tumour but tried to remove as much of it as they could. Babs had several more fits and was given medicine to control this. She also received chemotherapy and radiotherapy but continued to slip away. Peggy would return each night to a darkness that would reach into the deepest recesses of her mind and snuff out even the faintest glimmer of light. It was always "only one more drink." As the family sat around the bedside, all they could do was pray. For an end to the suffering, the pain, the fear, the guilt. It was time for Babs to go. Her eyes still closed, she tried to say something, but the words just wouldn't come. Finally, she sank back into her bed, her face radiating a calm and forgiveness that signalled a departure that was dignity in death. They remained in silence for what seemed an eternity, never to forget the lady who had brightened their lives. The light, the hope, the wind beneath their wings.

No one could ever imagine that losing a sister would not be a formidable obstacle to continuing her unobstructed passage through life. But it had hit Peggy hard. Very hard. She had fallen off the wagon and been thrown back into a deeper chasm than before.

The funeral was on a much larger scale than Jim's had been. Babs was the sort of person who you wouldn't be surprised was known to all. Sixty-six is no age to be lost to the world and Bermondsey came out en masse as the hearse glided respectfully along The Blue, her two children and three grandchildren in the car behind. The coffin was decorated with white double chrysanthemums spelling out the word MUM. It was a familiar sight to Dr Hither during his home visits, as he would wait for processions of black limousines and cars driven by other friends and family to pass before he joined the streets again. If he was walking along the pavement, he would stop and hold his head down in respect as the hearse passed by him. It was her dying wish that Babs be buried as Brockhead cemetery. The service was as traditional as Babs would have wished. Peggy knew that she would find it all too much, particularly when the first hymn was sung.

"Dear Lord and Father of mankind,
forgive our foolish ways..."

The music was stirring and uplifting. Peggy thought about what she would like sung at her own funeral. *Onward Christian Soldiers,* she thought. Yes, that was it. She would want Pat to read the eulogy. If not Pat, then Rene.

"...reclothe us in our rightful mind;
in purer lives your service find,

in deeper reverence praise,
in deeper reverence praise."

But Peggy couldn't control how it had made her feel and left abruptly in floods of tears, asking for a taxi to take her home. Rene spotted her leaving and mouthed an "It's OK" to Pat, pointing to herself, then to Peggy across the aisle, before leaving in hot pursuit, trying not to make too much of a scene as she did so. Their black dresses and coats still on, they sat in pin-drop silence amidst a cold emptiness that could not be warmed by heat from even the heartiest of hearths. Peggy didn't like anyone to see her drinking, least of all Rene. She concocted a reason for Rene to leave, without appearing rude or ungrateful. No sooner had the door snapped shut, Peggy opened her only source of comfort. This time, no tonic. Just neat. It took her back again. Right back.

"MOTHERS. Send them out of London." The bold blue poster was emblazoned with a stark warning of possible invasion and the threat of heavy bombing. It was September 1939. "Give them a chance of greater safety and health." The girl in the poster couldn't have been much older than Peggy. She'd been told that they could be going anywhere. They couldn't afford to go to where the posh people sent their children. Places she'd only heard about in story books – Canada, the United States, South Africa, Australia and others she didn't know existed. Peggy was only six and the other two knee high to a grasshopper. It meant that Mum could go with them. Peggy's mum had packed the necessary. Vests, pairs of knickers, socks, dresses and lots of handkerchiefs. Then the toiletries. A towel, soap, toothbrush, comb and facecloth. A mackintosh and plimsolls. For the journey, sandwiches, nuts, raisins and biscuits, apples and barley sugar sticks. All set for a new life, but The Phoney War meant a temporary return, only to start the whole journey again to somewhere new the following year at the same place in Devon. When the first call for evacuation was made, children were sat out on rush mats and red double decker buses would ferry them to different stations. Peggy's mum was waiting for them outside the school gates, with Pat and Babs.

After stepping off the specially commandeered bus and cutting through the early morning mist to enter Paddington station, this early start would later become a familiar sight to Peggy when the family would go hop picking after the War. For the moment, its multitudinous throng was suffocating as Peggy held on tightly for dear life to her mother's arm; the others clasping each of her hands. Although accompanied by their mum, each of the girls had been labelled like parcels, in case of accidental separation. Peggy watched the children who'd be travelling without their mothers, shivering with worry, not knowing even if their siblings would be travelling with them. She heard the chatter. "Mummy, I'm scared…I 'eard there's tigers in Devon…Do we get good grub where we're goin'…" It was a long journey that felt like the other end of the world, let alone the country. She didn't recall how long but long enough for all the food to be gone by the time they got there. It was another bus to the village hall, where children would be kept with their brothers and sisters. There, they were met by the billeting officer who would coordinate the 'pick-your-own evacuee' session. It was clear that the children were judged on their appearance. *How superficial is human nature,* Peggy thought, even then. Their mum with them, they were chosen first, probably because they were going to be 'low maintenance'.

Peggy worried that the children who looked grubbier and sicklier would be chosen last, but she wasn't around long enough to know. She tried to look for Rene, but she was nowhere to be seen. Her last memory was of children sitting in rows, their identification labels and boxed gas masks draped around their scrawny necks, wearing berets, cloth caps and knitted tank tops, with a glass of squash or milk in their hands, fearful of what lay ahead in a new life away from family and friends and their stay with strangers.

As their car crunched across the gravel in the remote Devon countryside, Peggy gazed in awe at a house that looked more like a palace. "Blimey, Peggy luv, it's like a mansion, ain't it?" her mum exclaimed. They shared it with three other families. By families, that was three lots of brothers and sisters. There were twelve of them in all, with their mum being the only accompanying parent. Staying there for five years was like one long holiday in the countryside. She would often hear her mum talking to Mrs Waddicombe, the lady who had taken them in and comparing the area to Paddock Wood and East Peckham. Place names that would trip off Peggy's tongue in her teenage years. By the time they left, Babs had started going to the local village school. After returning to Bermondsey, each girl had picked up the West Country drawl, as well as terms such as 'grockle'. They would all be teased for phrases that gave away their earliest formative years.

"Oi be Peggy, Oi be" and "'tis gettin' dimpsy." How she made her class laugh, slowly returning to her glottal stops and diphthongs. But never rhyming slang. That was for the East End, not for Bermondsey!

Peggy woke up muzzy-headed, groggy from the quarter bottle of gin that she'd consumed. She was on the floor but couldn't remember how she'd fallen. The television had been on since she'd got back at two o'clock and it was past six. She clambered up, using the radiator as support, her body aching from being sprawled out on the floor for who knows how long. Her right leg had gone to sleep. She winced at the pins and needles as the circulation returned to her foot. As she passed the mirror in the hall to go to the kitchen, she noticed a big purple stain all around her right eye. She checked for any bumps on her head. *All in one piece,* she thought. After the first glass of water, she still felt thirsty and gulped down a second. It was nearly time for dinner, but she really didn't fancy eating anything. There was a still the remnants of sardines from the day before, which she hastily put between two sliced of wholemeal, together with half a tin of cold baked beans. The food moved painfully down her throat, as she felt each mouthful crawl towards her stomach. She'd been told that she had a hiatus hernia, but this had become inflamed by her drinking, making eating even more painful.

On returning to her chair, she poured herself another drink. *No sense in calling the doctor,* she thought. There was nothing wrong with her. Just a bit stressed from what had happened to Babs. Who wouldn't be? What's the harm in a little drink now and again anyway? It certainly hadn't done her any harm. She would soon realise that denial would be her own worst enemy.

Peggy tried to hold things together as best she could. It didn't take Pat and Irene long to put two and two together, but they didn't say anything for fear of upsetting her. Between them, they had started to take over various household tasks such as getting her shopping, cleaning and this time, even doing the laundry. Pat would, with Peggy's permission, draw out fifty pounds per week to pay for shopping and give the rest to Peggy. Thankfully, all her amenities were paid for by direct debit. By the time the next week came around, Peggy would have spent it all on booze. Surprisingly, her mood didn't seem to dip, as it had done after she first started drinking when Jim died. What had changed was her memory. Even when not intoxicated, she would forget where she put things such as the remote control or her medicines. She also started having problems working the microwave or the cooker, that is, on the rare occasions when she used them. This was mostly at the behest of Pat, who would literally stand over her while she went through the motions of cooking and heating a hot meal with great reluctance. Peggy rarely went out, not even to Bingo. She'd stopped this completely when Pat had taken her shopping and then lost her way around, having to ask passers-by how to get back to her flat. Some kind soul eventually took her home and Rene had let her in, on hearing Peggy's voice. Pat had become so concerned, she had contemplated calling the police, until she'd had the good sense to check back at the flat. Peggy had forgotten where she'd been and appeared not to have a care in the world. When her memory problems first started, Pat thought that Peggy was doing it on purpose and would ask her to "behave like an older sister", which naturally left Peggy angry and upset. There was also something else that wasn't quite right. Peggy started becoming more stubborn, irritable and, yes, more awkward. She wouldn't do this with people such as Michael or the postman, but Pat and Rene would feel the full force of Peggy's new-found wrath. That was another thing. Peggy had started swearing. Not just mild cussing, but language that would make a sailor blush. The sort of parlance that Cyril would have used, but perhaps only after the few drinks.

"Peggy, do you mind, luv. Wash your mouth out!" was the reaction from a rather taken aback Rene.

But Peggy remained clueless as to why what she had said could appear offensive. It was as if the pause button was broken in her brain in saying what some would think of saying but would never say. Not ever. All her days seemed to merge into one. It wasn't long before Peggy would be set in a drinking pattern that would pervade her everyday routine like a creeping shadow enveloping her, insidiously, invidiously and without remorse. Alcohol is a complex molecule that can find its way into any person and take over their lives. If alcohol were to be put forward as a drug treatment today, it wouldn't even get past the first hurdle. Yet it remains legal, accessible and, even for Peggy, affordable. It was not a friend, but a foe. Not an angel but a demon. Not a tonic but a toxic chemical with considerable scope for harm. Within three years of losing Babs, she would be drinking at least a quarter bottle of gin a day. Her drinking was out of control and she often felt guilty about it. She could no longer do what others expected of her. Worse still, what she expected of herself. There were times that she literally couldn't remember what had happened when she'd been drinking. The concern from Pat and Rene often escalated into heated arguments, ending with them storming out of Peggy's flat. Pat's patience wore thin. After a particularly heavy drinking session, Peggy threatened to report Pat to the police for trespassing. The last straw was when Peggy had threatened to report her to Social Services for emotional abuse. That was it, Peggy had burned her last bridge of sisterly support. Pat withdrew, leaving a beleaguered Rene to take over, often at the expense of her home life.

There were days when Rene would visit and be so concerned that she would call an ambulance, but Peggy would refuse to go to hospital. Rene would plead with the staff to take her, but they would deem her as being able to make a rational decision to refuse treatment.

Dear Drug and Alcohol Team

RE: Mrs Peggy Lighterman (d.o.b. 7 March 1933)

I am becoming increasingly concerned about Mrs Lighterman. Her husband died from lung cancer two years ago and she lost her sister to brain cancer a year later. She has presented with frequent falls over the past few months but has refused to attend A&E.

Her last admission to hospital was in 2003 when she given a diagnosis of depression and harmful use of alcohol.

She has hypertension and a gastro-oesophageal reflux disorder but has not put in for a repeat prescription for some months.

Peggy's sister (Pat) had been helping with some domestic activities of daily living but has recently withdrawn all support following a progressively fraught relationship with her sister.

It is difficult to gauge how much Peggy drinks, but it is clearly impacting on her quality of life. Her recent blood results show evidence of alcohol related liver damage and her

MCV remains raised, in the absence of any other underlying cause.

The current presentation is different from the last in that I don't think that she has depression. Rather, she has been showing evidence of cognitive impairment. Her friend and neighbour (Rene) contacted me in confidence and told me that Peggy has locked herself out of her flat when going to buy alcohol, lost her way around the neighbourhood and has begun to say unkind things and behave in a manner that is very unlike her. Surprisingly, there are no marked word finding problems, which points away from a diagnosis of Alzheimer's Disease but I wondered about other types of dementia.

Yours Sincerely
Dr Arnold Moorse

The Drug and Alcohol Team wasn't used to seeing older people with alcohol problems but wrote to Peggy, nonetheless, offering her an appointment to assess her at their community team base and bring someone for support if necessary. It was standard practice. People using the service would then usually attend groups or one-to-one support at the same team base. There appeared to be little scope for home visits or ongoing support in a home environment.

As soon as Peggy saw the words 'drug and alcohol' on the letter, she threw it straight in the bin. She'd begun to realise that although she may have a problem with alcohol, what she feared most was how she would be judged by her friends and family. Even by her doctor. She couldn't control her drinking, but in no way, shape or form was she an alcoholic. Her dad was a proper alcoholic. Someone who got drunk, aggressive and died from damage to his liver. She didn't get drunk; she didn't hit people and to her knowledge, she wasn't going yellow with jaundice. Old women like her couldn't be alcoholics. Or at least that's what Peggy believed, together with a sizeable proportion of health professionals and most of the public. Alcoholism was lying in the middle of the street on a Saturday night in a state of paralytic inebriation. It was vomiting in a gutter, with a half-eaten kebab and chips strewn across the pavement. It was having a punch-up on a Friday night after one too many. It wasn't something that made you fall over, sick with worry, live like a prisoner in your own home or forget where you put the TV remote control. It wasn't Peggy. Denial is a blindfold that helps you to continue living the lie that is alcoholism. From that first drink, to the "what's the harm in one more?" to the escalating consumption, the need to drink to stop the shaking and finally the last act in a charade that leads to an untimely demise. But there is always an opportunity to intervene.

To be free from the shackles of impoverished solitude. That time was here again for Peggy but the die had been cast and Peggy's fate would be determined not by what is meet and right but by the arbitrary politics of every clinical practice. It was to be a shocking indictment of how the maintenance of petty boundaries were to determine her future. We had failed her. After a few attempts at engaging Peggy by letter and telephone, the drug and alcohol team wrote back to her GP, including the following lines:

"...we have not been able to engage with Peggy, either by telephone or letter and are discharging her from our service.

As there are concerns about her memory, I would suggest referring her to the memory service."

Dr Moorse was at his wits' end. Peggy was a human being, not a football to be kicked around between services. He wasted not a minute in referring Peggy to the memory service, using the same letter. A response came back in the form of an email, stating they had "looked carefully" at the referral and discussed it in their multidisciplinary team meeting. They had decided, on the advice of the consultant psychiatrist, that they "would not be able to make a valid assessment" unless Peggy had been sober for at least 3 months. Dr Moorse was seething, his hand shaking as he read the response.

When he had been called to see Peggy at home after she had fallen but refused to attend hospital, she was not intoxicated and was able to engage in an assessment that was sure to provide meaningful findings. How could they sit there and make snap judgements about *his patients*, his patients, without at least clapping eyes on them? So, he just kept going. Neurology. The same response. Neuropsychiatry. The same again. By this time, several months had passed and the number of home visits to see Peggy had become at least monthly. She had, by now, stopped all her medication and gave Dr Moorse short shrift whenever he visited. "Don't waste your time on me, Doctor. There must be plenty of others who need your time more."

Dr Moorse thought hard. Peggy's main problem was certainly alcoholism, but she was also beginning to lose her memory. It was a long shot, but he thought that he would try again. Another referral to the Community Mental Health Team for Older People. He kept his fingers crossed. As before, there was a reply from the Community Mental Health Team within a week. They were concerned that Peggy was still drinking, but also noted that she'd developed problems with her memory that required their expertise. The Team offered to see Peggy at her home and wrote a letter to her to that effect. As the letter fell onto her Welcome imprinted doormat, Peggy was sure that she'd seen such a letter before. Her instincts proved to be right. Sure enough, it was confirmation of a home visit. There was no mention of Dr Hither's name, so she called the Team herself. It didn't take long for Peggy's heart to sink.

"What do you mean Dr Hither doesn't work there anymore?" She was seized by a sense of disbelief.

"I'm sorry, Mrs Lighterman, but Dr Hither has retired."

The silence on Peggy's side of line was one of anguish. "He's the only one that knows me. Surely, he'll see me if I ask him nicely?" Peggy was now imploring.

"I'll check but I don't think he sees patients privately." The voice was empathic and soothing but offered Peggy no reassurance.

"But he must. He must!" Peggy started to feel another outpouring of despair. "I'll see if we can contact him Mrs Lighterman and will let you know if we do."

Dr Moorse called Peggy to find out the state of play. He was not at all surprised over Peggy's reaction to the news. He had immense respect for Dr Hither, who would go the extra mile for his patients, particularly those with alcohol problems, even though his was not a service for people with alcohol addiction. Peggy waited. Days, then weeks, then months. There was no sign of Dr Hither and Peggy was beginning to give up hope.

Chapter 9
The Public Good

Dr Theo Hither, MBBS. The certificate from West Cross Medical School, initially taking pride of place in his study at home, was now gathering dust in a box somewhere in the attic. Along with other certificates of achievement, he had never seen the point in displaying them. Hugely influenced by his school ethic and 'Christian' values, he would much rather be judged according to what he had done for society rather than anything else. A strong ethical code had meant his ready departure from any encounter or relationship, be it professional or social, where he was expected to turn a blind eye to the rules. Being labelled as someone who played "straight down the line" did not also go down well with those who wanted to bend the rules for convenience. There was a strong sense of meritocracy about his approach to life. He had got where he was through sheer hard work. No silver spoon. No Masonic Lodge or secret handshake. Not anti-establishment, just pro-justice.

Working in Bermondsey had only reinforced the simmering sense of social justice that even transcended the boundaries of his clinical practice. His mother was a teacher for children with special educational needs and instilled in him a strong sense of perseverance in what she called the "Robert the Bruce" approach to life. "We have a lot to learn from spiders" she would tell him whenever he would give up on a task. She also taught him an even more valuable lesson. One of opportunity.

Like many teachers, she strongly believed that the reason why children appear not to understand or learn is because the teacher is not doing their job properly. It would stand Theo in good stead for the rest of his career. There is always a solution. Always a way around a problem. His interest in psychiatry had come early in his life when his mother had given him a book on Psychology. He learnt about the different models of behaviour change through the work of Skinner. The concept of conflict and the unconscious mind. Most appealing of all was human behaviour and what made people 'tick'. It was an invaluable foundation for his progress into medical school. The psychology and sociology components of his course in medical school would absorb him. The way society labels people with mental illness struck a chord with him, having been sensitised to this by Adam's mental health problems. You can't see it, but it is still there and difficult to put into words. That's mental illness in a nutshell but it's the mental pain that it most difficult to understand. All you can do is try and put yourself in someone else's shoes and that's far from easy. So many steps in the winding staircase to recovery, Theo reflected. Recognising that there's a problem, seeking help, engaging with treatment and sticking with treatment. All steep steps to climb without the right help. Then there's stigma. There's always stigma.

As a psychiatrist in training, Theo had completed a post in the psychiatry of learning disability. He remembered his mother calling it Mental Handicap as he was growing up. The newer term was a more fitting description. At the time Theo was in post, the large psychiatric hospitals were closing, and patients were placed in the community. For people with learning disability, it was a double whammy. It was about getting used to living outside institutionalised care where care was done to them not with them. But it didn't help that local residents would be up in arms over what the press called the Not In My Back Yard or a NIMBY response. If there's one thing that Theo detested more, it was the normalisation and integration of people with learning disability meant people having to bear the ignominy of being stared, pointed and smirked at in public. What if it was their son or daughter? Their mother or father? The boot would be on the other foot. It was not until he started a training post in the psychiatry of older people that he had unlocked the door to a different world. Here was a group of people who had been largely overlooked by society. Their problems were often hidden behind closed doors. They usually had multiple problems. Ongoing physical problems such as stroke and Parkinson's; social adversity such as not being able to get out and about or manage their everyday care needs and the added burden of mental illness.

Apart from mental disorders such as depression, anxiety, bipolar disorder and schizophrenia that could affect people of any age, dementia was more common in later life. Theo was stimulated by the range of skills needed to be able to offer the best care. The old age psychiatrist needed to be proficient in assessing the nervous system. To carry out a physical examination. To conduct an in-depth assessment of memory and other intellectual functions. To assess a person's mental capacity to make an informed decision about care. That was still only a part of the wider picture of working with families and carers, as well as assessing and managing someone's risk at home and balancing this against living independently. No two patients were alike. Challenging but rewarding. It was a rude awakening using these skills to work in Bermondsey. Dr Hither's patients mostly lived in deprivation and with multiple physical, mental health and social problems. It was the public good that Dr Hither sought above everything, so that unmet need should never remain unmet. The influence on his philosophy in life harked back to his years at King Edward the Martyr and the words of St Ignatius of Loyola.

"Teach us, good Lord to serve thee as thou deservest,
to give and not to count the cost;
to fight and not to heed the wounds;
to toil and not to seek for rest;
to labour and not to ask for any reward;
except that of knowing that we do thy will
Amen."

The influences in his life were indeed unique. The strong ethical code ingrained in his personality from childhood, his mother's work ethic and never-say-die attitude and his brother's mental illness had all made him the person that he was. He had done his best by Peggy and many others before her. It was the cruellest twist of fate that he would leave the streets and homes of Bermondsey without the peace of mind that Peggy would be safe and secure for the rest of her life. As he hung up his boots, Dr Hither took one last look at a community whose spirit would never be vanquished. It had been home to many a docker, street trader, printer and factory worker, whose trades had disappeared. He had tried to change the world, if only in a small community that would never give up. There had never been a place quite like it and probably never will. Bermondsey would always be great.

Chapter 10
The Pledge

Long before he knew Peggy, Dr Hither had been aware that the drinking culture in Bermondsey was influenced by the life of dockers, whose drinking habits persisted well after retirement. It wasn't long before another piece of the jigsaw was put in in place to explain why it was that the area had become such a hotspot for drinking in older people. The only difference being that the drinking culture of the Irish community in Bermondsey couldn't have been more different. Michael had many stories to tell of his and his parents' life, as well as that of the Irish community and the role they played in shaping Bermondsey over the centuries. He had told Rene stories of how the Irish potato famine in the 1840s had led many people sailing to St Saviour's Dock near Tower Bridge, an area of huge deprivation around what was known as Jacob's Island. Jacob's Island had a reputation of having the worst slums in the country but it is a sad fact of life that it was also the only place where the new population could afford to live. Over an open fire and with several children to keep occupied, Michael's mother would sing ballads. Her favourite was *Poor Pat Must Emigrate*.

"Oh, farewell to poor old Erin's Isle, I now must leave you for a while

The rent and taxes are so high, I can no longer stay

From Dublin Quay I sailed away and landed here but yesterday

My shoes and brogues and my shirt are all that's in my kit

I've just called in to let you know the sights I've seen before I go

Of the ups and down of Ireland since the year of '48

And if our nation had its own

Our noble sons would stay at home

But since fortune had proved otherwise

Poor Pat must emigrate.

Yet, the new population remained marginalised, that too in one of the poorest areas of London with a notoriety that remained unsurpassed. It was almost exactly a century later that a fresh wave of migrants made the same trip. The men would work on the roads and railways and women in service. Apart from areas such as Manchester and Liverpool, Bermondsey was one of the three areas of London where Irish families settled. The others were Kilburn and Hammersmith. It was this population that had set Dr Hither on a career path from which he would never look back. The Irish men whom Dr Hither saw as patients had, like the dockers, not changed their drinking since retirement. They would remain socially isolated, remaining largely within their own cultural circles, drinking together and working together.

They had survived rather than thrived, coming to South London to be met with signs in the landlord or landlady's window of "No blacks, no Irish, no dogs." To be put in the same category as dogs was an insult too far. As they grew older, many had lost friends and relatives to drink at an even younger age than the dockers. Michael had been one of several families that had taken The Pledge in their younger days. During his confirmation, Michael had sworn to take The Pledge, a concept developed in the late nineteenth century by the Pioneer Total Abstinence Association. He had the pin to prove it. At the other extreme was Dr Hither's caseload of patients. It would not be too far from the truth to say that over one in ten of his patients were Irish and all, without exception, had a problem with alcohol at some time during their lives. He was starting to see an ever-growing number of older Irish men whose alcohol consumption had affected their memory, and many had dementia. That was a turning point that turned the tide of Dr Hither's approach to his clinical practice. Never again would he turn away patients who had mental health problems that included drinking problems.

Michael had remained on the straight and narrow in avoiding the excesses of booze, but he was not completely teetotal. He and Rene would still have a glass of wine with their meal if they went out for special occasions such as birthdays and weddings. And the not-so-special ones such as wakes.

Michael's mother had succumbed to the perils of drink, but for a different reason. She had been brought up in poverty, with ten siblings, her father a farmer in County Clare. He knew that his mother had suffered with her nerves, but kept it hidden. It wasn't so easy to keep her drinking hidden. She would, in modern parlance, be called a functioning alcoholic. It wasn't so much the strong smell of gin or the shakes, but more of a mother who struggled to get through the day.

Michael was the second eldest child, with a sister, Eileen, ahead of him. He would come home from school to find his mother sleeping or complaining of just not feeling well. It wasn't long before he and his siblings ended up running the house. His father would come back home and shout "Eileen. Have yous been on the lash again?" Cycles of poor mental health and childhood adversity perpetuate through the generations until someone has a lucky break. A confidante, a kind relative or maybe even a bright child who escapes the hamster wheel of deprivation. Eileen suffered emotional abuse as a child and grew up with such low self-esteem, her coping skills were easily decompensated. When all the children had left home and Michael would go and visit his mother in Ireland, she was still drinking. He was convinced that, had she been born in these times, her alcoholism would have been spotted early and she would have received the support that she needed.

Instead, she was addicted not just to alcohol, but to downers and smoked 40 a day. The last time he saw her, she hadn't been out of the house for a year. The doctor had told her she had agoraphobia. She would cough every time she tried to speak, a persistent fruity cough that almost shook the room, such was its force. He was surprised that her lungs and kidneys hadn't given up the ghost. That is until she died from cirrhosis. Alcoholism and mental health problems had led her to an early grave at the age of just sixty-two.

Chapter 11
The Lights Go Down

It had been well over a year since that fateful call to Dr Hither's team. By this time, Peggy's drinking had stepped up a notch. The worst time of day was on waking. She would feel queasy and would vomit but nothing would come up from the horrible and incapacitating heaving. She would feel a sickly kind of panic, her heart beating like the clappers. Noises would bother her. The sound of the kettle would be like a jet taking off in her kitchen. Being unable to sit still for more than a few seconds, she would pace around frantically, but nothing would calm her. The only thing that did was a swig of gin. That settled her down immediately, but she started needing more of it to achieve the same effect. She would then start to use alcohol as a way of staving off her withdrawal symptoms rather than as a quick fix to drown out what had become a pathetic existence. "The person has to want to change," Rene had heard from her own GP, when she expressed concern over Peggy's drinking. But how could a person living a lie called alcoholism ever change? Rene had asked herself this question countless times, but it's a circular rhetoric that led nowhere in seeking a solution that could drag her closest friend out the pit into which she had fallen, deeper and deeper. Peggy was now barely visible as a person. There was still the odd flash of the old Peggy, but it was soon beaten into submission by the booze. Like Alice falling down the rabbit hole, there seemed to be no limit to the depths to which Peggy's drinking had reached. So, she did what many might consider the best course of action but would be sadly mistaken. She stopped drinking suddenly one day after she'd run out of gin. Rene had been visiting less and less and was on holiday with Michael, so no one was there to raise the alarm. The same day, she suffered a fit. Somehow, she had managed to come to without any complications that she could see, but over the next few days, the horrors were soon upon her. She felt as if she was burning up, with the most bizarre sensations in her body. It could be anything from itching, burning or numbness to a feeling as if bugs were crawling under her skin. She would hear her name being called, saw shadows that moved and sometimes snakes seemed to come out of the lampshades. It was bizarre but frighteningly real and very constantly terrifying. At just after midnight, she called Pat in a panic. Because of her memory problems, she had become unable to remember Pat's number and always seemed to be mislaying her address book, so she'd bought herself a telephone with a speed dial function. Shaking uncontrollably, her finger could barely press the dial button. Pat knew that something was wrong. She was the last person Peggy would want to call after their fallout. "Pat, they're here." Peggy had started to believe that there were intruders in her house.

"They are, Pat. They're bugging the place. How did they get in? I didn't let them in. They've put snakes in my electricity meter, Pat. They are vile people. Please ask them to leave Pat, please. It's nearly lunchtime. I have to go to work tomorrow and Jim will be home soon."

There was no mistaking that Peggy needed help, and fast. Pat called an ambulance and put a coat over her nightie. It was cold, bitterly cold. After scraping a thin layer of ice from the windscreen and making several attempts to frighten the ignition into submission, she was on her way to Peggy's flat, arriving on the Chuzzlewit Estate at the same time as the blue lights of the yellow and green striped vehicle in front or her. The lifts were working this time. A relief for the ambulance staff and for Pat and Michael.

"Hello, Peggy, I'm Catherine. Can you tell me what's been happening?"

"You're not my niece. What are you doing here?" Peggy was emaciated, her nightgown filthy and food stained; her hair long and matted. Her lips dry and cracked. She appeared anxious and agitated, pacing around, pointing to the ceiling as she did so. "They're in there. They're in there." There were so many empty bottles strewn across the carpet, that there was barely space for Catherine and her co-worker to move around.

"It's the ambulance, Peggy. The ambulance. They've come to take you to hospital."

Peggy's eyes lit up. "Well, get me out of here then!"

After being lifted into a wheelchair, it wasn't long before the latest drama was over. Pat called her husband on a mobile kindly supplied by Catherine and accompanied Peggy in the back of the ambulance to their destination.

The roads were icy as they passed a gritter lorry, its yellow flashing lights mixing with the ambulance's blue to form, for an instant, a green swirl that whisked the early morning Bermondsey air.

Her mind and body driven relentlessly to the point of exhaustion and calmed by the medication prescribed to ease the symptoms of alcohol withdrawal, Peggy slept with an observable serenity that would obfuscate any passing patient, doctor or visitor and cause them to ask the question "she looks so well." The corners of her mouth turned up into a fixed smile.

"Ging gang gooli, gooli, gooli, gooli, watcha
Ging, gang, goo, Ging, gang, goo,

Hey-la, hey-la shey-la
Hey-la shey-la, hey-la ho-o-ooo."

It was hard for a London girl adjusting to the rustic rural life of Windborough Sands. But Peggy was not alone, as evacuees such as her were not an uncommon sight in the playgrounds of Devon during the early 1940s. She missed Rene and her other friends dearly and girls can be quite cliquey and unforgiving. But Peggy was fortunate that the warm-hearted far outnumbered the mean-spirited and she soon made friends. Some with whom she would keep in contact, but most from whom she would simply drift apart. Mrs Waddicombe was always superficially pleasant to Peggy, but not always to the other children under her care. Peggy was sure that her mum would soon speak out at the slightest hint of rebuke. In a spirited effort to fit in better, she joined the Brownies. She later recalled someone telling her of how Lord and Lady Baden Powell founded the Scouts and Girls Guides respectively and how Daisy Gordon Low founded the erstwhile Rosebuds of the Great War; soon changing to the

Brownies and named after the 'helpful creatures' in Lady Baden Powell's favourite story book. The whole Brownie experience was more like something from a children's adventure and she loved it to bits. Every Wednesday, she and three other girls would walk to the local club, a hop, skip and a jump from the house, catching a delightful sea view along the way. Her first day was a little daunting, as she held up her hand to recite the familiar pledge of allegiance. Very different to saying Grace before dinner. It was strange. Peggy's mum wasn't religious. Neither was Cyril for that matter. But they both insisted that they should always be grateful for what they were about to receive. She conjured up images of Mr Bumble's intimidating figure standing over Oliver Twist or Wackford Squeers over Smike as she knelt in front of her peers.

"I promise to do my duty to God and the King and to help other people every day. Especially those at home."

She wore her Promise Badge with pride, the pre-War trefoil now replaced by an elf, nymph, sprites or gnome.

Peggy puffed out her chest like a peacock as she pinned it to her uniform. It was a symbol not just of her promise to do good but as a bond of camaraderie. She was deadly serious about her pledge to the world, with a fierce competitiveness that she would never lose. She even passed her First-Class Test – a proper assault course for mind and body. Cleaning knives, forks and spoons. Cleaning boots and drying them, even when wet. Making dolls' clothes and a Brownie overall. Folding clothes for the mangle. Knitting socks or wristlets. Applying a triangular bandage. Knowing and showing different types of physical exercise. Making a milk pudding. Even remembering a twelve-word message in case this was needed, as part of the War effort. All those memories and some of the best days of her life. Peggy was indeed fortunate to have a family whose goodwill extended far beyond their instructed role. Seeing the film *Snow White and the Seven Dwarfs* was a rare treat. The children would spend endless hours playing Monopoly and Peggy would always want to build a hotel on the Old Kent Road. Imagine that. A hotel in Bermondsey, she would tell herself. A proper posh bath with clean water and someone to come and serve you roast beef and ice cream! There were other treats, which she would later miss but cherish forever. Crisps with that small blue packet of salt inside that she would empty into the packet and shake. 'Walking the dog' with a yo-yo. Distant but treasured mental mementos. Peggy was in a different world when she joined the Girl Guides. Never in the limelight, she would prefer to sing the accompanying verse to complement the frothy exuberance of the Hey-la shey-la chorus.

"Shalli-walli, Shalli-walli,
Shalli-walli, Shalli-walli,
Oompa, oompa, oompa, oompa."

It all went by so fast and by the time she had returned to her beloved Bermondsey, she was a little lady of twelve.

When Peggy awoke, her bed felt like a warm cocoon, the mattress gently caressing her back as if she was floating on the ripples of the ocean. The lights were turned down to their lowest level. Peggy felt different. She zoned in on her body and took a snapshot. No shaking, no sickness, no sense of inner restlessness. Just calm and relaxed. Those young people today would probably say 'chilled out' or 'in the zone'. Her clothes were clean, and she felt safe and comfortable. But something was different. Where was she? A sudden wave of goose bumps washed over her. Had she been kidnapped? She looked around. What were other people doing in her room? So many people. She hadn't invited them.

"Help me, please. Someone help me!"

Hearing the commotion, a nurse came running.

"Peggy. Whatever's the matter?"

"Officer, please get these people out of my bedroom. They shouldn't be here."

The nurse in charge, Donna, was on her first shift since qualification and wasn't sure what to say or do. She went to call the shift coordinator, Indira.

"Peggy, everything's OK. You are in hospital. I'm one of the nurses. Can I get you a glass of water? Let me know if you need to use the toilet."

Peggy's screwed up her eyes as Nurse Indira turned on her bedside light.

"I don't remember asking to come here. Anyway, who did you say you were? A police lady or something, wasn't it?"

Indira sat with Peggy for a little while, explaining again why she had been brought in and that she was on medication to help her through her alcohol withdrawal.

"I barely touch a drop these days. I don't get time to drink, what with getting my shopping, paying the bills and going to the West End. Drink was the death of my father and I certainly don't want to end up in an early grave." Peggy rolled up her eyes and shook her head. "I'm going to sleep now, so please turn off the light when you go."

The next morning, Peggy awoke to the hubbub of the morning shift. Nurses moving into and out of bays, taking recordings, a cleaner mopping the corridors, food trolleys hauled around and doctors moving frantically between beds to check drug charts.

A bit like Waterloo Station, only this time with doctors and nurses as drivers and guards and patients as passengers. Peggy still didn't know where she was. Perhaps it was a hotel, but a very busy one. A tray of breakfast was placed on her bedside table. There was orange juice, porridge and toast, with a small tub of jam and portion of margarine. She wasn't hungry but it did seem a tad rude to refuse if the kind lady had gone to all the trouble of bringing her breakfast in bed. Peggy smiled politely. When the melee had died down, Peggy heard a familiar voice.

"Peggy. Oh, Peggy, luv. You're looking better already. How are you, luv?"

Peggy didn't take long to remember her best friend but had no recollection of her having been on holiday. Rene thought it best to keep mum. She soon recognised that Peggy was having problems recalling recent events and focusing on their conversation. Although she was able to find the right words when speaking, she repeated herself a lot. She also found it hard to keep a constant flow of words and would occasionally shock Rene by some of her comments about people around her.

"Look at that lovely man (pointing to a student nurse). If I were fifty years younger, I'd like to…"

"Shhh, Peggy! Not in here, luv. This is a hospital." Rene blushed and diverted Peggy onto another topic.

"I hope Pat and Babs are all right?" Peggy had clearly forgotten the death of Babs, the acrimonious parting with Pat, and her involvement in Peggy's admission. Pat nodded in the affirmative. "I tell you, Rene. I still miss Jim. I do, luv, I do." Jim's death appeared to have created a flashbulb memory, not uncommon for emotionally charged events. When Pat had left, Peggy would call out for the nurse, asking where she was and why she was there. No amount of repetition made a difference. Her alcohol detox complete, arrangements were made to transfer Peggy back to Ada Salter Ward.

The ward hadn't changed much. Some staff had moved on, but Ade was still there. Peggy did not recognise what would have been previously familiar surroundings and faces. A large vacuum had been left by Dr Hither's departure, but life goes on and his replacement, Dr Hughes, was now the incumbent consultant.

Thursday, 10 March 2005
NURSING ENTRY

10.07 Peggy arrived on the ward, accompanied by a friend (Rene). We attempted to contact her next of kin (Pat) but there was no answer. Rene informed me that Pat has now made it clear that she doesn't want any contact with Peggy and is happy for the mental health team to make any decisions about her care.

Rene kindly offered to take on this role and we have taken down her contact details. We have taken receipt of Peggy's clothes, toiletries and list of medication, which we will check with her GP.

MEDICAL ENTRY
11.04
New Admission
Peggy Lighterman (d.o.b. 7.3.1933) 124 Cratchit House Chuzzlewit Estate London SE1 1LM

Mrs Peggy Lighterman is a seventy-three-year-old widow, admitted from Hedley Perkins Ward at St Saviour's Hospital today, following an episode of delirium tremens. She was found at home following a call to her sister.

She believed that there were people inside her flat and reported seeing snakes coming from the lampshade. She was treated with oral medication as part of a detoxification regimen, together with high dose parenteral thiamine. There is also a history of progressive cognitive decline, with short-term memory loss and personality change.

At interview, Mrs Lighterman did not report any problems with her memory or her mood. She was unable to provide a clear account of recent events, stating that this was her home and that she was getting annoyed about people coming in and out all the time.

She was admitted to St Saviour's Hospital in January 2003 following a fall but was discharged the same day. Over the next few months, she presented to her GP with non-specific symptoms, for which there was no physical aetiology. Mrs Lighterman has a history of HT and GORD. She is on a calcium channel blocker and proton pump inhibitor (see drug chart) but has been non-compliant with both these drugs for at least twelve months.

Her mother died at the age of 85 from bronchitis and her father from alcohol related liver disease in his early 50s. She is the eldest of three siblings. Her younger sister (Babs) died from a glioblastoma last year and her other sister (Pat) lives in Bermondsey, with no contact.

Mrs Lighterman was assessed by the Bermondsey Community Mental Health Team for Older People in September 2003 and a diagnosis of a depressive episode was made. She was started on an SSRI and reviewed a month later, at which time her depressive symptoms had worsened.

She was admitted to Ada Salter Ward but was discharged within a few days following a sudden improvement in her mood. She was followed up at home by Dr Hither, Consultant Old Age Psychiatrist, but her mood deteriorated again, and was re-admitted to Ada Salter Ward. On the ward, she was found to have withdrawal symptoms and underwent alcohol detoxification, which included parenteral thiamine. Her mood improved, but she was found to have mild cognitive impairment, possibly associated with harmful use of alcohol. She was followed up in the community by the CMHT and received a package of care, which was stopped after a few weeks. She was then discharged from the CMHT in October 2003.

In her alcohol history, she drank alcohol no more than monthly, usually 1–2 units, until her husband died in 2002. Her alcohol use disorder was missed following the fall in 2003 and during her admission to Ada Salter Ward later that year.

Her GP had referred her to the drug and alcohol service in March 2004, when there was evidence that harmful use of alcohol had progressed into dependence, as well as possible worsening of her alcohol related cognitive impairment. However, she failed to engage with this service and was not taken on by the memory, neuropsychiatry or neurology services, all of whom would not assess her if she was not abstinent from alcohol for at least three months.

She was then referred to Bermondsey CMHT for older people but would only see Dr Hither, who had, by then, retired. There has been no contact with mental health or addiction services until her current admission.

In her social history, she lives in a thirteenth floor two-bedroom council flat with lift access. Her friend (Rene), to whom I have spoken, reports that Peggy was fully independent with everyday activities until her mental state deteriorated following the death of her sister in January 2004, when she started drinking more heavily. She has not been managing her finances independently and we have found from Rene that her telephone line was disconnected through non-payment and she is in arrears with her gas and electricity. It is estimated that she has been drinking between 40 and 50 units of alcohol per week over the past twelve months, with an accompanying decline in cognitive function.

Before admission to Saviour's Hospital, she was found in a state of self-neglect and her flat has since been found to be infested with bed bugs and mice. There was out of date food in the fridge and several empty bottles of gin around the flat.

Several falls have been recorded, but she has consistently refused to have them investigated. She is independently mobile, wears glasses for reading and there is no hearing impairment.

In her pre-morbid personality, Mrs Lighterman is described as outgoing, makes friends easily, has previously helped coordinate activities at her local Tenants Association and had a wide social circle. Since the onset of her alcohol dependence, her only contact has been her friend Rene.

On mental state examination, she was a thin lady dressed in a yellow top and white dress, with adequate self-care. There was no clouding of consciousness and no marked change in her psychomotor activity. Her affect was irritable, and she was markedly disinhibited, asking me if I was born here and what my parents did for a living. There was no evidence of depressive symptoms, or abnormalities in thought or perception. On cognitive testing, she was disorientated for day, date, month, season and year; as well as for address, borough (gave the answer as Bermondsey, rather than Southwark) and city.

She was able to register three items but could not recall any of these after thirty seconds. Concentration was poor, but language skills were preserved. She was able to comprehend a written command but unable to carry out a three-stage task or copy intersecting pentagons. When asked to write a sentence, she wrote "Don't ask me such stupid childish questions."

On frontal lobe testing, she was only able to name four animals in a minute and there was evidence or marked perseveration. Her abstract thinking was also impaired.

On neurological examination, there was no evidence to suggest stroke or Parkinsonian signs but there was evidence of cerebellar dysfunction, in keeping with her history of alcohol use disorder.

My impression is that there is evidence to suggest both alcohol use disorder which coincides with the onset of dementia. The relative preservation of language and impairment in frontal lobe function suggests alcohol related dementia.

PLAN

- *Involve Rene in admission planning meeting*
- *Order head MRI scan to gauge the extent of alcohol related brain damage*
- *Continue high dose oral thiamine*
- *Routine blood investigations*
- *Routine physical observations*

Dr A Khan SHO in Psychiatry

NURSING ENTRIES

14.10 Peggy had a light lunch but only ate half of it. Fluid intake was 250mls. She was able to feed herself independently with a knife and fork and there were no problems with swallowing.

17.10 Peggy was seated in her room. I introduced myself as having been her nurse when she was here before, but she did not recognise me as Ade, Instead, she thought that I was her 'home help'. Peggy asked me to clean her room because she had guests coming. When I repeated that I was her nurse and that she was in hospital, she became irritable and told me to 'go back home, where I belong'. Her friend (Rene) looked upset and said that Peggy would not usually say things like this. I said that I quite understand. It is not Peggy's fault when she says these things. I said that to Rene that she is always welcome to come and speak to me and I will try and help as best I can. I recorded her vital signs. Temp 36.7, Pulse 80, BP 150/100, Oxygen Sats 98%.

NIGHT STAFF NURSING ENTRY
Friday, 11 March 2005

07.00 Assisted Peggy with washing and dressing. She was able to wash herself independently but put her clothes on the wrong way around. She became angry when we tried to offer to help, but we eventually managed to assist Peggy to change into her nightclothes. Peggy did not sleep well. She asked why there were people in her house.

She became irritable when I tried to assist her back to her room, but I left her for a few minutes as she walked around and then came back to her, asking if she would like a cup of hot chocolate, which she gladly accepted.

Peggy was then escorted back to her room at about 3am, where she remained settled and slept. Remains asleep at the time of report.

Monday, 21 March 2005
Ward Round Notes
Present
Dr Raz Hughes, Consultant Old Age Psychiatrist
Dr Izzy Snape, Registrar
Bryony Cape, Ward Manager
Sam Kantalia, Occupational Therapist
Jack Musowicz, Psychologist
Sandra Owen-Jeffries, Social Worker

Dr Snape presented Mrs Lighterman's history, highlighting the onset of regular heavy drinking following the death of her husband, which was missed through services not asking about alcohol intake.

This has included her admission to Ada Salter Ward, when no formal diagnosis made. Dr Snape went on to describe how, during a home visit, Dr Hither had made a diagnosis of depressive disorder and had only discovered Mrs Lighterman's alcohol consumption by chance. She then showed evidence of withdrawal symptoms during admission and underwent alcohol detoxification. During the admission, her mood improved on antidepressant treatment and she was discharged with a package of care and follow up by the Bermondsey Community Mental Health Team. The package of care was stopped after a few weeks and the CMHT continued to review her, eventually discharging her to primary care. Throughout this time, Mrs Lighterman had remained abstinent.

She had refused any psychological therapy, saying that she would think about it. Similarly, she did not want to engage with drug and alcohol services, as she wanted to be seen at home and was happy with the input provided by her Community Psychiatric Nurse. However, this meant that she was not able to develop ways of managing any early warning signs or cognitive behavioural techniques if she were to start drinking again. She relapsed in her drinking following the death of her sister. When her GP started noticing evidence of cognitive impairment, she was referred to several services, all of which refused to assess her if she was drinking. She eventually presented with full blown delirium tremens and was admitted to a medical ward for detoxification.

At interview, Mrs Lighterman was unable to give a clear account of recent events, believing that she was in her own home and that other staff and patients were 'lodgers'. She was not aware of the nature of her memory problems or the extent to which these have affected her everyday life.

Dr Snape spoke to Rene, next of kin, who confirmed the history above, also adding that there had been considerable decline in what Peggy could do for herself, she had begun to neglect her hygiene and was eating hardly anything at all. Rene had stopped buying alcohol for Peggy, but Peggy had managed to persuade other neighbours to do this. She had also asked neighbours whom she did not know to do this.

Rene had started to notice that Peggy, even when not under the influence of alcohol, had become more stubborn, irritable and awkward, with a 'short fuse' and 'would fly off the handle for no reason'. She had also started to swear and make personal comments, which was very unlike her. Mrs Lighterman's unsatisfactory social circumstances were described and it has recently been discovered that £2,000 had gone missing from her account. Social Services are currently investigating a safeguarding referral in connection with a "friend" named Selina, which Rene knew nothing about.

The history of hypertension and gastro-oesophageal reflux disease was noted, as was non-compliance with medication.

Dr Hughes noted the absence of tobacco use and there is no past or current use of prescribed or illicit opioids, cannabis or other illicit drug use disorders.

Mental State Examination on 19 March

Appearance and Behaviour

There was marked irritability and, at times, verbal aggression. Rapport was difficult to establish. There was also suspiciousness, agitation and restlessness, telling the doctor to "stop being such an idiot" and "get out of my house." At times, she would raise her fist, but not hit out.

Speech

Speech was reduced in flow, with constant repetition of the same stock words and phrases.

Mood

There was no evidence of self-reported low mood or other depressive symptoms and no hopelessness or suicidal ideation.

Thoughts

There were delusions of theft, secondary to memory impairment. She believed that people were coming into her room, moving her things around and stealing her possessions and money.

Perceptions

There was no evidence of any perceptual disturbance such as hallucinations.

Cognitive Function

Would not allow this to be tested formally, but the presence of impaired memory, visuospatial and frontal lobe function was noted. Ward staff report that she is disorientated in time and place, with frequent verbal aggression during personal care but surprisingly still remembers the names of her sisters and her friends. However, she has been verbally abusive to Rene when she has visited and, one occasion, pushed her such that she fell over but did no sustain any injuries.

Physical Examination

Pulse 80 and regular. Blood pressure 160/100. No abnormalities on cardiovascular or respiratory examination. On abdominal examination, mild hepatomegaly but no ascites. On neurological examination, no gait abnormalities and normal power, tone and reflexes. No signs of Parkinsonism but signs of cerebellar impairment.

Blood investigations

Raised MCV and Gamma GT, low albumin.

Head MRI scan

There are marked changes in white matter but no infarction or haemorrhage. Moderate cerebral atrophy, most prominent in the frontal lobes. There is marked cerebellar atrophy, particularly in the central region. An area of cerebral softening is noted in the left frontal lobe, likely to be associated with traumatic brain injury.

Formulation

73-year-old widowed lady with 3-year history of alcohol use disorder, starting as harmful use following the death of her husband, escalating into dependence. There was a period of 6 months' abstinence and independent living, but a relapse following the death of her sister. No single service felt able to assess her and she refused contact with the older people's mental health service following the retirement of Dr Hither.

Over this time, there was deterioration in social function and interpersonal relationships, with worsening self-neglect, falls and poor nutrition. The rapid cessation of drinking culminated in a withdrawal fit and delirium tremens. Mental state examination shows evidence of severe cognitive impairment, with considerable impairment in frontal lobe function. There is limited insight into the nature and severity of her cognitive impairment, and she lacks mental capacity into decisions affecting her living arrangements, health care, finances and general affairs. On physical examination, there is evidence of alcohol related liver disease and alcohol related hypertension, as well as alcohol related brain damage in the form of cerebral and cerebellar atrophy. There is also evidence of traumatic brain injury from repeated falls. Blood investigations show poor nutrition and alcohol related liver disease.

PLAN

Monitor blood pressure and other routine observations daily

Monitor mental state and behaviour, including compliance with medication and nursing interventions, mobility and falls, sleep, mood, food and fluid intake

Continue high dose thiamine

Encourage ward activities and arrange occupational therapy assessment to gauge level of independence

Wednesday, 6 April 2005

Nursing Report (Night Staff)

Daily verbal and physical aggression continue and are worse at night. Offered Peggy a cup of tea, which she threw at my colleague, telling us to get out of her room. Remains resistant to personal care, hitting, spitting, scratching and kicking. Offered time out, with some success when more settled, but behaviour remains challenging for staff. Offered medication to lessen agitation but spat it out. Eventually settled and slept at 4am after walking up and down the corridor looking for her husband, asking why he's so late back from his night shift at the hospital.

Peggy sat in the patients' lounge against a cushion that made her back ache terribly. Her primary nurse had suggested that Peggy sit with the others. She fixed the other patients with a steely but glassy eyed stare and leaned over to Bert, who was sitting next to her. "Jim, luv, get us a cup of tea, will you." Her eyes reflected some vague recognition of her former years. Her dear Jim was departed but her mind was fixed in time. Bert didn't reply. Too pre-occupied by his own guilt and past failings. Self-absorbed, miserable and wretched. A shadow of his former self as the fine upstanding dock foreman who would count the men into groups before they departed for piece work. A man who could belt out an impressive rendition of *Fly Me to the Moon* when the booze had had hit that sweet spot. He swirled in an abyss of depression, caught between Scylla and Charybdis of despair and desolation. He wasn't to know, in that dark lonely place, that, within a few weeks, his depression would be treated. Back down the pub and the betting shop. Back driving his motor. Back to his wife. Back to life.

Peggy just shrugged and rolled her eyes. "Please yourself, you lazy git!" Her eyes turned to the TV screen, watched by countless others before her. Some had experienced remarkable recoveries. But sitting there in what was a wilderness of emotion, many could not even begin to contemplate how their lives would change for the better. At a time that they did not live-in hope; hope was something given to them but the doctors, nurses, psychologists, occupational therapists, support workers and many more who had faith in the treatment offered by mental health services.

Peggy detested the presence of so many people in her flat. Jim was welcome but no one else had been invited. No one. Why were they eating on her table, sleeping in all her rooms, using her plates? Her cutlery? Peggy wasn't paying for their food. No fear. Or their gas or electric. She had a good mind to call the police. That would sort them out once and for all. Maybe Rene, Pat or Babs could do something. Where were they when she needed them. Daytime TV was no different in hospital than at home. It was soporific. She drifted off again, to a world with no people behind screens. Just children behind dreams.

"Bluebells, cockle shells
Eevy, Ivy, Over
Bluebells, cockle shells
Eevy, Ivy, Over.

Mum is going down the Quay
Coming 'ome at 'alf past three
Getting bread for lunch and tea
How many slices can you count?

1, 2, 3, 4..."

It was Peggy's turn and she jumped as if her life depended on it. Each time, she would close her eyes and imagine that she could rise and touch the sun.

That she could see forever, as she drifted effortlessly above the smoke-belching factories of Drummond Road, the leather market, the print works, all part of the beating heart of Bermondsey. And then down on the hard, concrete floor, between the whirling rope, ready to carry her up again with its *swish, swish,* swishing current of whistling air.

Peggy still preferred Tin Can Copper. She was always the last to be caught as the children spread across the road like a blanket, determined to probe every nook and cranny in search of that elusive last person, so that they could continue their game afresh. It was always Billy Hurley who found her. She was sure that he would end up being a policemen or detective, or one of those people on a secret mission. The alarm rang out in a shriek of excitement.

"Tin Can Copper, I spy Peggy Lighterman hiding behind the post box pillar…"

Billy was always first back to kick the can before you could say Jack Robinson. It just wasn't fair. As she passed into the land of One Potato Two Potato and Teddy Bear Teddy Bear, she sat bolt upright as the ward sprang into action.

"Lunch, Peggy. It's lunchtime"

Peggy awoke from her playground slumber, more disorientated than usual. She wasn't best pleased being taken away from her friends. "I hadn't finished playing. It's not even dark yet." Why were there so many old people around? Where had all her children gone? No amount of cajoling was going to get Peggy Lighterman in before the sun went down. So, she sat tight, hoping that, at any minute, she would hear the background hum of chatter and giggling, shouting and crying, moaning and groaning. The sweet lullaby of somnolence carried out into an ocean bobbing with memories. Her eyes closed again.

"Run, Peggy, run!" The sky above swarmed with Focke-Wulf 190s as a ten-year-old Peggy was out on a field trip from Castlecombe School in Windborough Sands. Having set off from Caen, the fleet was en route to launch an attack on Bournemouth that would live long in the memory of both the people of Hampshire and Dorset. The air raid siren was deafening, and the children scattered in all directions. There was no air raid shelter in sight. As Peggy ran for her life, she came across an elderly man, who gesticulated wildly, pointing to a nearby wall.

"There! Behind there. Quick! Be quick!"

Like William Webb Ellis touching down his first try, she dived behind the wall, as the bombs rained down with an ear-splitting whistle and a final thunderous boom, churning up concrete and spraying it in all directions, as it ricocheted off buildings and vehicles. She lay there motionless on the cold muddy path, shaking and sobbing uncontrollably. After a few minutes, the air raid siren faded, and she stood up to see swathes of rubble as buildings had been razed to the ground in the wake of the relentless shelling that had engulfed it. It was a day that was branded on Peggy's memory. The village had lost its soul that fateful day, together with the lives of two children and five teachers. Life had chosen her, and she vowed to cherish it even more.

Peggy awoke in a more content frame of mind and made her way to the dining table. Today, roast lamb, mashed potato and green beans looked more appetising than usual. She might even try the jam sponge and custard.

Monday, 25 April 2005
Ward Round Notes
Present
Dr Raz Hughes, Consultant Old Age Psychiatrist
Dr Izzy Snape, Registrar
Bryony Cape, Ward Manager
Sam Kantalia, Occupational Therapist
Jack Musowicz Psychologist
Sandra Owen-Jeffries Social Worker

A Best Interest Meeting was held. Rene did not attend and passed on the message that she is willing to accept any decision made by the ward, although also stating that she did not feel able to provide support to Peggy, were she able to return home. Mrs Lighterman requires personal care for washing, bathing and dressing and supervision with medication. She requires prompting with toileting and is at risk of urinary incontinence and now wears pads. There is also a risk of falls. Prompting and supervision is also needed for feeding but she can use cutlery appropriately and able to drink from a cup or glass independently. She is not orientated to a daily routine such as meal and medication times and will lose her way to and from her room if not directed. Her behaviour remains disinhibited, with daily episodes of irritability and verbal aggression. She is also physically aggressive and racially abusive during personal care interventions.

Low dose psychotropic medication has lessened her agitation, but the risks of increasing the dose outweighs any benefits. There have been almost daily verbal altercations with other patients, mainly women, whom she accuses of 'stealing' another patient from her – a man whom she misidentifies as being her husband. She has also been more unsettled over the past three nights and was found to have a urinary tract infection that is now being treated. On the first night, when acutely disorientated and agitated, she asked if her baby was all right and appeared markedly tearful. As she has gradually been regressing back to her younger days, we wondered if she had been pregnant and possibly suffered a miscarriage. Her medical notes do not mention this and there is no one in her family that we can ask.

Chapter 12
Silence

Peggy was in the pink. Everything was going swimmingly once she and Jim had settled into the routine of living away from Mum, ensconced in their modest fifth floor council flat on the Bellamy Estate. They were slightly further away from the Blue than when at Mum's flat, but still near enough to feel part of the community. The buzz of Bermondsey that made you feel that you belong. With Peggy teaching and Jim on the docks, it just seemed like the time was right for dear Peggy to be in the family way.

Contraception wasn't exactly an everyday dinner table topic, but a fact of life. There were the throwaway remarks from Peggy's mum. "You'd better get cracking, Peggy luv, unless you want to be a granny before you drop a sprog."

Jim nearly choked on his pork chop when he heard that less than poetic utterance, although to be fair, one too many Babychams had loosened her tongue more than she might have liked. Peggy and Jim hadn't wanted to hear the pitter patter of tiny feet until they were older than most. Who knows why? Maybe it wasn't wanting to burden Peggy's mum while they were living with her. Maybe it was about having more money in the coffers. Who really knows? Peggy had tried just about everything going. The cap, the coil and then the Pill. It wasn't until she was 32 and Jim 37 that they decided to make a go of it. Peggy had always wanted to be a mum. It was something that just felt right.

So, when she missed a period and sallied forth to the doctor's surgery off Jamaica Road, it was surely the beginning of something very special. Peggy had heard that in the USA "they put your wee into a frog to make it lay eggs", or at least that's what her friend Gladys had told her, who had heard it from a friend of a friend. Anyway, there wasn't such a thing as a pregnancy test when Peggy went to her doctor on that clear but chilly Spring day in 1968.

Dr Clackton was indeed a man of few words. The sort of man that might be better at looking in your ears or taking your temperature or blood pressure. Always quick with the pen to scribble an illegible prescription, but less adept at communication. Peggy knocked on the door, gingerly, anticipating the usual "Enter!", followed by a "Well, what seems to be the matter?" The room was as clinical as it could be. The good doctor's certificates neatly lined up on the wall above his desk. A tarnished silver framed picture of his wife and child, obscured by a layer of dust. On his desk, a prescription pad that looked as if he had spent hours aligning with a spirit level so that it was plumb with the edge of the wall. A skull and some other funny looking bones on top of a locked cabinet. Peggy joked with Jim that he kept his Dr Jekyll mask in there, which he used to scare the children if they became too fractious, or if they "gave him the 'ump" as Babs to aptly put it. But Dr Clackton had a heart of gold.

He was always ready to visit his patients at home, to check how they were and would even visit his patients in hospital.

Of course, there would be no curling of the corner of his mouth. Just being there was enough for his patients. Peggy felt under the stone cold, wooden seat and pulled the chair closer to the doctor.

"You see, Doctor, I've missed my time of the month." Peggy was perhaps a little more reserved about these sorts of things than Babs or Pat. "It's been six weeks. I think I might be…"

"Hmm." He had never looked at her directly. It was almost as if, in his own Dr Clackton way, he may even have been excited by the news. "Lie down on the couch if you would, Mrs Lighterman." He looked out of the window as he prodded her tummy. "No, nothing that I can detect." Peggy was half tempted to say something more fitting for Babs, such "what did you expect to find doctor? A leg of lamb? The Mona Lisa?" But, she didn't and went on her merry way to wait it out and return in another month. When she did, she was given a slip to go to the antenatal clinic at St Botolph's Hospital. Now knocked down to make room for a block of flats. Then, a thriving cottage hospital in the heart of Bermondsey. By then, she knew it for certain. The morning sickness had started, and she would find herself having to rush out of the classroom to heave into the staff toilet. The doctor gave her the news that finally meant she was on tenterhooks no longer.

But she only told her nearest and dearest and hid her baby bump as well as she could. Underneath it all, was natural excitement and expectation. It had to be a home birth, where you knew your midwife. It just seemed like the 'right place' to have a baby. A small cot, a rug to make the room look that bit comfier.

By the time she knew it, the quickening had started and she remembered the song *I knew an old lady who swallowed a spider. That wriggled and jiggled and tickled inside her*. It was coming up to her second term and she continued to work and would do until she was ready for the big arrival. There was no paid maternity leave and continuing to work in the later stages of pregnancy was back breaking, not to mention the frequent trips to the loo. But someone up there had decided that for Peggy, motherhood would be a pipe dream, never to be fulfilled.

She sat on the toilet and wiped down below, only to find that there was blood on the tissue. Peggy froze and, for an instant, so did time. An infinite number of thoughts churned inside her head. But she was trapped. Not sitting in her toilet at home but in the staff toilet, opening into the main staff room. She wiped again. Still more blood. Not exactly a gush, but a trickle and enough to raise alarm bells. She then realised that, although she hadn't said anything to Jim, she hadn't felt any movement in her tummy for a few days. That feeling that made you feel uncomfortable but tells you that there's another life inside you.

It was lunchtime and she could hear the hum of conversation from the nearby staff room. Peggy panicked, pulled up her knickers and skirt and sprung out into the staff room, puzzled faces all around her. She didn't have time to look around, her heart racing. The headmistress happened to be in her line of flight and noticed Peggy's demeanour.

"Peggy, whatever's wrong?"

"I need to get home. I need to get home. I need to get home…" Her voice was tremulous, her body shaking uncontrollably. She had a flashback to the bombing raid, causing her to double up and curl into a ball on the floor.

"Come on, Peggy, I'm taking you home." Mrs Grainswell was the only teacher with a car, parked at the back of the school in a locked garage. Peggy didn't utter a word on the way back home. Only a "thank you" as she scurried from the car, forgetting to close the passenger door as she did so. "Let me know when you're ready to come back" were Mrs Grainswell's last words.

Peggy fumbled with her keys, dropping them several times, then putting the wrong one in the door, eventually succeeding and almost diving onto the settee, sobbing uncontrollably. Once she had gained some degree of composure, she called her mother, who was there in an instant. They sat together, through several tissues and several hours.

When Jim got back, it didn't take long for him to work things out. Peggy, her mother and Jim went to St Botolph's Hospital and she was seen by the doctor. Peggy had always found it odd that doctors who saw only women patients were almost exclusively men. But he was calm and gave her time to talk. He confirmed her worst fears. This was a miscarriage and she was likely to have more and heavier bleeding over the next few days while the foetus came out. He was right. The cramps and bleeding started almost immediately. Peggy felt an emotional numbness and detachment, still denying to herself that this could have possibly happened to her. On the third day, she felt something plop into the pan. It looked like a small purple sack and she knew that it was her dead baby. What should she do? Take it out? Leave it there? Her dead child floating in the water. She flushed the toilet, her head spinning. Over the next few days, she was clearly on a short fuse. Why me? What have I done wrong? Is it something I did, or didn't do? Should I have got more sleep? Eaten more? Eaten less? Got more exercise? She was chasing her own thought tail. A week later, she was entertaining a different stream of emotion. Why couldn't I have died, and that poor innocent baby lived? She would have gladly given her life in return. Peggy moved in with her mother for a few weeks, feeling exhausted and wretched. Her doctor gave her some tablets for her 'nerves', but she didn't like taking tablets.

She discovered several years later that many women of her age became addicted to these tablets, which people knew as 'mother's little helpers'. By this time, she had lost two stone in weight and at times felt so low that she felt like ending it all. That was how bad she felt. She couldn't explain it to anyone. They just wouldn't understand. But Mum did and surprisingly, so did Jim. Her doctor gave her a different type of tablet, which he said was for depression. They made her feel sleepy and gave her a dry mouth and constipation, but whatever they did, they seemed to work. Within a few weeks, she started to feel the black dog no longer clinging to her. Although the loss had left a deep emotional scar, she was beginning to accept that she needed to get on with her life. The loss of her baby would be something she never talk about and somehow, never got onto her medical records. She would live with this secret and when her mother and Jim were gone, it was hers. Only hers.

Peggy returned to work but didn't try for any more children. Jim had the 'snip' and they never spoke about their loss again. Perhaps they should have and perhaps Peggy should have sought professional help. The stiff upper lip, 'grin and bear it' days meant that for many, like Peggy, their loss festered inside them, only to re-appear in some other form at some other time in their lives. The stage seemed to be set for Peggy.

Everything laid out along the slippery slope that would lead Peggy to self-destruction. Her fate was sealed.

Chapter 13

Salad Days, Autumn Nights

There remained a feeling of community in 1980s Bermondsey, although it was fast disappearing. There was one big difference between the Lightermans and other regulars on a Friday night out. Whereas Jim's friends at his local would be drinking each other under the table and Peggy's at the Bellamy Estate social club would be more than a little merry, if not lairy, neither Peggy nor Jim would get so much as mildly tipsy. That's not to say that they didn't feel like party poopers as those around them talked more loudly and less clearly as night progressed, swaying like a loaded barge approaching Canada Dock in choppy waters as they ordered the next round. They had both seen what drink could do and could recount stories that would make your toes curl, of how drink could drive you into an early grave. Although they enjoyed a knees-up as much as the next person, they were now approaching middle age. Like many of their friends, it was down by the coast that suited their social life better. Jim had decided to buy a car when he started at St Saviour's Hospital. Mainly so that, each winter and summer, they could visit their caravan down on the south coast. They probably spent half the year there until they both retired and would then set off further afield, to Europe. Caravans and their seaside surrounding were a slice of what home was like in the old days. It also reminded them of trips to the seaside when they were younger. The salty breeze. The cockles, muscles, winkles and whelks lightly garnished with sand. Fresh fish with your chips. None of that frozen stuff from the supermarket aisles. Peggy and Jim would walk towards the beach, where the activities in and around the pier would immerse them in another world. One of sandcastles, donkey rides, rock with your names running right through it, dirty postcards. Punch and Judy, candy floss and toffee apples. You might half expect to see Kolly Kibber's picture in the *Daily Messenger*, Pinkie and Rose walking arm in arm or Colleoni's men jumping Spicer in the darkest recesses of the pier. In their caravan park, gone were the days of do it yourself entertainment with a microphone and doing your turn as if you were on New Faces or Opportunity Knocks. It was now all Karoake and lip-synch, even if you wanted to sing Buddy Holly, Elvis or the Rolling Stones. Sometimes they'd be lucky to have old bands touring the caravan parks. Bands like The Searchers, The Fortunes, Marty Wilde, Joe Brown, Freddie and the Dreamers and The Ivy League. Booze had become all trendy, with lager replacing Watney's Red Barrel and Alcopops the new sherry. If it all got too high-tech, they would retreat to the caravan, where they could watch their old favourites on video cassettes. Their favourite was *The Italian Job and Alfie*, mainly because the leading role was played by none other than their Maurice Micklewhite or Michael Caine as he was more commonly known.

He was born just a month after Peggy and from their very own Bermondsey. Jim loved the old classic comedies.

Hancock's Half Hour, *On the Buses*, *Steptoe and Son*, *Till Death Us Do Part.* Unlike Dr Hither, who was still donning his white coat as a medical student at the time, they never quite got into *Blackadder*, *Monty Python* or *Yes, Minister.* They liked their humour served to them less bizarre and more straightforward. Although Peggy did once laugh out loud at episodes of *Reginald Perrin* whenever CJ opened his mouth and kept saying that he never got where he was today without doing or saying this or that. As for Dr Hither, his life couldn't have been more different. As a baby boomer, he had been born into the world of colour television, bubble gum, space hoppers, conkers, clackers, Action Man, Scalextric and Subbuteo. No social media meant that just like Peggy, children played outside at every available opportunity. Kicking around a half-deflated football that would always continue to leak no matter how many times you pumped it up, using jumpers as goal posts and doing a victory dance as if you were Geoff Hurst in 1966. Pushing yourself so far forward on the swing that you could almost touch the top bar. Is that what a bird feels like? Playground slides never got boring even at your umpteenth descent. Keeping caterpillars in a metal tin with holes, in the vain hope that they would metamorphose into butterflies.

Swapping football cards but finding that your friends also had the same defender from Uruguay who you were sure they included in nearly every packet. Summer evenings riding Raleighs or Choppers around until dusk was upon them and it was time for supper. Dr Hither's early life was probably more like Peggy's than both of them would ever know. Both brought up on working class estates with straight talking people and a sense of community. It did, in no small way, augment the "Christian" values of Dr Hither's school to firmly inculcate the firm belief that the real world is hidden from the public. It is a world where need is great, but help was scarce. But for him, he was to have a life less ordinary. He would not squander it, but he also wanted to leave a legacy of having contributed towards making the world a better place. The world would be the judge of that.

Peggy and Jim's sojourns to the caravan began to peter out when they moved to the Chuzzlewit Estate in the late 1980s. What started off as a group of like-minded companions with shared living space, where the only inconvenience was the dog from next door's caravan howling at the moon, merged imperceptibly into holidays spent next to neighbours with posh caravans. Not the dockers or bricklayers, but the nouveau riche builders, the estate agents or car dealer with a caravan filled with the latest cooker or television. It wasn't the same place. But Bermondsey was also changing apace.

Moving to a different urban sprawl on the Chuzzlewit Estate in 1988, Bermondsey just seemed to re-invent itself into yet higher concrete blocks covering an even larger area. They saw blocks being demolished and converted into luxury flats sold at several times the price paid only thirty years before. It was fast becoming a forgotten community. Overseas investors were now absentee landlords. Markets downsized or closed. The High Street became unrecognisable. Pubs were flats. The underpass disappeared. There was more glass than concrete, but it wasn't Peggy and Jim's glass. It was never their glass. The biggest change? The streets were deserted. The lure of the television screen, the DVD, the mobile 'phone and the computer had curtailed the outdoor buzz of learning through socialisation. Rough and tumble had become virtual reality. In and hidden was the new out and about. We will never know if Peggy's life after Jim would have been different had she been living in the Bermondsey of her youth. The saddest part of all is that Peggy's mind had become an almost blank slate. All she had now was her memories.

Chapter 14

A World Apart

Monday, 23 May 2005
Discharge Planning Meeting
Present
Dr Raz Hughes, Consultant Old Age Psychiatrist
Dr Izzy Snape, Registrar
Bryony Cape, Ward Manager
Sam Kantalia, Occupational Therapist
Jack Musowicz, Psychologist
Jayne Leggitt, IMCA
Apologies: Sandra Owen-Jeffries, Social Worker

As no next of kin was present, an Independent Mental Capacity Advocate was in attendance. This is a new role under the 2005 Mental Capacity Act, where an independent advocate is appointed to make decisions in the best interests of the patient.

Mrs Lighterman has been an in-patient for 2 months. She remains disorientated for time and place and it is difficult to engage in activities. However, she responds to music during ward activities run by the OT and enjoys singing and dancing to music from her younger days. She remains agitated and can be both verbally and physically aggressive during personal care. Her appetite has improved but she sleeps poorly at night, more recently asking where we have taken her child and becomes acutely distressed.

A form has been completed for fully NHS funded continuing care, given the unpredictable frequency and intensity of her behaviour, non-compliance with medication and the recent diagnosis of diabetes mellitus. There is also now both urinary and faecal incontinence and she is at risk of falls through instability. It was agreed that Mrs Lighterman lacks mental capacity over decisions affecting her living arrangements, health care and finances. This is based on her inability to retain, recall, use and weigh up relevant information.

PLAN

- To be transferred to Bluemere Continuing Care Unit next week
- Discharge summary completed
- Nursing handover to be completed
- Maintain input from Occupational Therapy Psychology and Physiotherapy after discharge
- To maintain monitoring of weekly temperature, blood pressure, oxygen saturation and blood glucose
- Continue with medication for hypertension, GORD and diabetes mellitus
- IMCA to remain involved in care on discharge

Bluemere had such a different feel about it. The soft pastille colours on the wall. Pictures of Bermondsey from bygone days. One of a tram on Tower Bridge Road. Another of the Astoria Cinema. Posters of old films. It felt nostalgic to relatives who visited, many of whom also commented on how blissfully calm and unhurried the whole ethos of care was towards its fifteen residents.

Even Peggy's behaviour became somewhat less agitated, as if she was breathing tranquillity itself. Her problems remained but staff always seemed to find a solution to overcoming them. Being a specialist unit, it had two big advantages. Adequate staffing and adequate time in which to carry out their nursing. Peggy would carry around a doll, which she would cling onto for dear life. Feeding Peggy meant little and often. She needed to be supported when walking around, so that she didn't take a tumble. Now and again, she would stop in her tracks when she saw something on television or heard music that triggered a thought, emotion or memory. She still spoke about having to go to work, to see Jim or to check on her mum. Medication would have to be given in her food and care would need to be taken to ensure that she was regular and not too bunged up. As she started to be become less mobile, a closer eye was kept on her skin care and regular physiotherapy to reduce the risk of developing contractures. She had taken quite a shine to both the male nurse and the male physio, with what you might call lewd comments about what she would do if she was twenty years younger! It was too late to wind the clock back, but what if things had been different? If people had worked together to help Peggy. Instead of languishing and suffering in silence, what if the response from all those services had been completely different? What then?

"...we have not been able to engage with Peggy, either by telephone or letter but are happy to see her at home. We will attempt to do this, as she may find this a more personable approach, although we appreciate that it might take some time engage her."

Dr Moorse was touched to see that so much attention had been paid and effort made to create a therapeutic relationship with Peggy. He knew that she would be a tough cookie but hoped that their perseverance would pay off.

Dave was more used to seeing people younger than Peggy, many of whom would be have been drinking heavily for most of their life. They had often lost their job, were estranged from their families and their health had suffered greatly. As with Peggy, they had seen their lives blighted by drinking. What once was a social pursuit was now a demon that had possessed them, determined to drive them to destruction. Dave didn't do many home visits. Most people came to him at the centre, where he would arrange a certain number of sessions to help them make the changes that they so desperately needed in their lives. The problem was that they were always in two minds, with the 'I can' and 'I can't', the 'I want to, I don't want to' in constant dialogue. Peggy didn't like change, but who does? Dave's visit had caught her off guard.

Strange, Peggy thought. *No one comes to see me.*

It must be the postman or someone. She opened the door, the latch still on.

"Can I help you?" Peggy blinked in the light. It was well past 11, but she was still in her nightie and wasn't really in the frame of mind to be making any polite conversation.

"Hello, Peggy, my name is Dave. I'm from the community team." He lifted his badge so that it was in her line of vision.

"I said that I don't want to see anyone apart from Dr Hither." She cast a suspicious eye over the unwelcome visitor.

"I don't work with Dr Hither, Peggy. I'm from the community alcohol team." He couldn't lie just to get a foot in the door. If Dr Hither had been there, he would have stories to tell about relatives asking him to say that he was from the council, to not upset the person he was seeing for the first time.

"Well, you can tell your boss that I don't want to see anyone." Peggy was defiant. She just wanted to go back in and have another drink and keep the telly on for company. "Sorry, young man, but you've had a wasted trip. Bye now." Peggy had opened the door, enough for Dave to peer in and take stock of the flat.

"I can see that your flat's in a bit of a state. Perhaps that's something we could talk about?"

"Well, I've got no hot water. They've cut it off. And the tap's leaking. Perhaps there's no harm in you having a look but I don't want to talk about anything else. Just the heating and the tap and then out you go."

Peggy pointed alternately to the flat and the street, as if she was playing a game of Eeny Meeny Miny Moe.

The flat had a musty smell, with thick layers of dust on the furniture and picture frames. There was paint peeling off the walls and a large patch of damp on the bathroom ceiling. The floors were sticky and the sink in the kitchen caked with grime. The warm weather had attracted flies that fed on the half-eaten food from a plate in her sitting room. The hall was filled with black plastic bags, filled mostly with polystyrene take away containers and empty bottles of spirits. It was an eye opener for Dave but not because he hadn't seen it before. He just hadn't seen and heard of an older person with Peggy's background living in such squalor.

"There's the tap." Dave had to step over two black bags to get to it. The tap was badly rusted and probably needed a new washer, if not replacing.

"Would you mind if I sat down?" Dave needed to be more than a handyman on this visit.

"Well, all right then, but I've got things to do. The housework won't do itself." Dave sat on the edge of a settee that was badly worn and covered with all manner of things that Dave didn't care to consider.

In the process, he stepped on what sounded like a piece of toast. It was a large cockroach. Dave flinched and became momentarily pale but gave nothing away to Peggy.

"Peggy. I can see that the flat's probably in a different state to, maybe, last year. Is there any problem that you might be having to make it more difficult for you to keep it how it used to be?"

"You try keeping this place clean when you have to do it all yourself." Peggy's denial was clear, but a conversation had started. It was the conversation of hope. The conversation of change. But Dave could not rush the process. There was a lot of work to be done and it had barely started.

"Perhaps we could start by me contacting the housing officer to see if we can get that tap fixed." Dave knew that getting the hot water back on meant sorting her finances and that would mean involving social services. It wasn't ideal, but that time would come. It just wasn't going to be now.

Dave rose from the settee and walked a little more slowly and vigilantly than when he had entered, not wanting to experience a similar cockroach encounter underfoot.

"What about the heating?" Peggy enquired.

"Perhaps we could get the tap sorted and maybe get someone to do a bit of clearing up. Maybe we could start with getting rid of some of those bags."

It is a common fallacy to believe that 'treating' someone simply means probing into their life, giving them a diagnosis, telling them what treatment they need and stop seeing them when they have finished their 'treatment episode'. But drinking is not like that. It is a behaviour where change involves a joint effort to achieve a goal. It doesn't just damage health, it destroys lives and how we manage all the components of our everyday existence that we take for granted. Cooking, laundry, shopping, cleaning, getting out and about, relationships with friends and family, eating, sleeping. Even feeling and thinking. It wasn't about the tap. It was about Peggy's life. A life that had washed away her soul, to be carried far out to sea on a tide of loneliness and hopelessness. After a while, it becomes a status quo and people start thinking "Oh, well, she's probably always been like that. She's a good for nothing drunk, feeling sorry for herself. It's pathetic. She's only got herself to blame."

When Dave visited the following week, he came with the housing officer, who said that she would get the tap replaced. Dave arranged for one of the agencies attached to the Council to get rid of the bags. Peggy found this more acceptable than having Social Services involved.

Any mention of this at the outset conjured up memories of home carers helping her to get dressed and she wasn't having any of that. At the third visit, it was time for Dave to look at what he could do to help Peggy change the drinking that had become her. But change talk would come at a price, with a journey into uncharted waters. She had to want to change, to feel that she could change, to see why it was so important to her. Not to Pat, Irene, or her GP, but to her. To Peggy. If she saw the need to change, she could commit herself to it and to say, "Dear world, I'm ready now and this is how I'm going to do it."

Peggy had been used to doctors lecturing Cyril that he should stop drinking or it would kill him. That was it. But it just made him even more defensive. It was someone judging him, reinforcing the stigma he already felt as an 'alcoholic' and telling him to do something he was not ready to do. There was always a part of him that wanted to stop, but the odds were always stacked against him. On the one hand, he knew that it was destroying his and his family's life. On the other, it made him feel better in the short term. Got him "out of 'is 'ead" as her Peggy's mum put it. It also made him feel part of society. A bond that linked him together with his peers that made it a hard habit to break. Besides, his trump card was always "I've known people live 'til they was ninety and they were drinking the same as me at my age." He knew but denied that this was the exception, not the rule.

Drinking is like a castle with the drawbridge raised and the moat as deep as it can be so that no one can come into your world. A world where you feel shame and guilt but unable to stop the runaway train.

"Peggy, your GP asked me to see you because he was concerns about your drinking. I wondered if you felt the same and whether I could help you to look at this. What do you think?" Dave's opening gambit was as non-confrontational as it could possibly be.

"Look, Mr…sorry, Dave. I'm fine just the way I am. I'm very grateful for all you've done for me with the tap and all that. But I really don't think it's any of your business what I drink or how much I drink. I'm hardly an alcoholic. Go and take a good look at those little tykes who stand outside the block and start causing a nuisance at night. All that singing and fighting. Cans everywhere, even in the corridor. They're the problem, not me, Dave. Not me."

"If you were to wake up tomorrow, Peggy, and everything was back to normal, as it was not that long ago. What would be different?" It was the golden question and it hit Peggy like a bolt out of the blue.

"Maybe I could get out to have my hair done more often. Get on better with Pat…" The drawbridge was coming down, letting in clean air, a sense of hope and purpose.

Over the next few weeks, Peggy started to at least contemplate how her life had been affected by her drinking. How it stopped her from doing what she could do before. How it had affected other people. Most important of all, what could happen if she didn't change her drinking habit. Dave even got Peggy to write a drink diary. She's always thought that a pint of beer and bottle of whiskey had the same amount of alcohol. Already, Dave had started to get Peggy to think about what parts of her life she could change. She was starting to be in control and Dave had helped her to see this more clearly. Peggy was asked to write reasons for and against drinking and she was surprised as to how many things appeared on the list of cons. Still, there were always the buts. "But it makes me feel better…but they say that there's no harm in drinking and may even be good for you…but…" By the end of the second month, Peggy had started to think about making changes to her drinking, but "only when I'm ready." The was the next big hurdle for Peggy and she often became stuck. That is until she was able to see for herself how she could do it. She could really do it! She could come up with a plan, with solutions to break the resistance.

And all along, Dave would engage her, with no expectations, no judging, no pushiness, talking with Peggy not to her, with empathy oozing from every syllable.

She felt valued, listened to and confident to start thinking about her future. A future that had been locked away in a cabinet of guilt and fear. So, Dave and Peggy sat down and worked on a plan. A plan that involved small steps, nothing too grand. Something that was achievable but working towards a better future. She started by cutting down her drinking by small amounts at a time. Dave offered her the choice of having assisted detox, but she wasn't at all keen. She could do it herself, she knew she could. She'd done it before, and she could again. Dave began to see an improvement in Peggy over the next few months. Her skin, her mood, her confidence. Each time she achieved that small step in her plan, Dave would feed it back to her positively in affirmations. The ignition to the Peggymobile had started to move her into action. She was soon down to less than half a bottle of gin a day, then a quarter. During this time, she felt clear-headed, got out more and had all her amenities restored. To the sheer dismay of her friends and even Rene, she was a different woman. Not a hair out of place, back with the necklace, the make-up and the earrings. Although she had seen Pat out on occasions when she was shopping, Pat would simply turn her back and walk in the opposite direction. Then, one fine day, she bit the bullet and waved a white flag.

We often cause more heartache to those closest to us than to anyone else. Families are strange beasts. They can even be beasts of burden to those within them. The emotional closeness gives us a carte blanche to act out in any way we see fit. We can confront our loved ones, safe in the knowledge that their unconditional love will buffer them from the hurt. But the mockery, anger, jealousy, suspicion, undermining, control and deviance can be the levers that prise families apart. Peggy did not mean to drive Pat away from her life and she could not bear to think of her only sister being a stranger to her for the rest of her life. So, she asked Dave to contact Pat himself and to let her know what transpired. When Pat did get back to Dave several answerphone messages later, she was still smarting from her last encounter with the elder child of what was now the terrible two. In fact, she even came to see Dave on her own at his community team. She wanted to put over her side of the story. For that to happen, there needed to be confidentiality, a validation of her feeling and a knowing that she was being heard and not judged. She needed to know what he could do and what he could not. To both Dave and Peggy's surprise, Pat agreed to meet with Peggy, but only on neutral ground. That ground was to be family therapy. There were some difficult moments when it started. That was to be expected. Pat would arrive at the dot of ten and make a quick escape when the session was over. The interaction between Pat and Peggy was fed back to them by members of what was referred to as the 'reflective team'. They made little eye contact when they spoke, occasionally casting furtive glances at the therapist, looking to him for approval. When the therapist's notes were complete, it was able to shine a light on what Pat was going through all those months when trying to support her sister. If truth be told, the emotional impact on Pat from Peggy's drinking was probably deeper than on Peggy herself. They were words that had the power to move mountains and they did.

"Peggy didn't care about me or anyone else. The ambulance was there so many times, I just lost count. I'd go home exhausted, sometimes having to get her into bed. It was like lifting a sack of potatoes. Looking after Peggy was like looking after a child. Sometimes she would wet herself or worse, and who was there to clean it all up? Muggins, that's who. Good old Pat. She won't mind picking up the pieces. She'll clean up your bloody mess.

"I'd always be on edge, waiting for someone from the surgery or an ambulance person to tell me that she'd fallen again and refused to go into the hospital. When it did ring, I'd be thinking if they were going to tell me that she had broken her hip, knocked herself out or worse. I don't know how she could do that.

"She only thought of herself, selfish cow. That kind and lovely sister I had. She lost every ounce of goodness. She used to snap at me, insult my husband, even push me. I was so scared of her. Of what she might do next.

"There was good old Peggy, leading the life of Riley while I went home after the ambulance crew gone at two in the morning, absolutely shattered with all my own work to do the next day.

"My life was in pieces. I started to get snappy with my husband. The things I said to him, it's a wonder he didn't walk

out. I got low, really low, but I couldn't tell anyone, could I? The shame of having a sister who's an alcoholic. I bet they knew though. I bet they was all pointing, saying it was my fault that I didn't stop her drinking. I was meant to be the strong one. The one who was there for everyone. But I'm a human being. I feel things just like anyone else. But when she said those nasty things, I thought that was it. She can clean her own mess, clean her own flat, make her own bed. I just couldn't do it no more."

They had heard what Pat had to say but Peggy also needed to be heard and her story delivered an emotional sucker punch that would leave Pat reeling. She would come to her senses to be more immersed in the life of an ex-alcoholic and with her support, someone would remain just that. Peggy, the sober ex-alcoholic.

"We never spoke about Dad's drinking. We just got used to it. Mum sometimes took a battering, and we would hide under the bed on a Friday night. When we saw her with a black eye the next morning, Dad would be all sweetness and light, cracking jokes as if nothing had ever happened. I'm sure it must have affected us all; made us more vulnerable. When I was older, Mum would confide in me about what Dad would do.

"He would force himself on her and I could hear her sobbing sometimes in the kitchen at night. She always said that it wasn't his fault, but her fault for being such a bad wife and mum. At least that's what he made her believe. When he died, it's like she had a new lease of life. She started seeing someone she met at the social club. She said he was such a

kind man. I never saw her happier. You can never choose your parents, can you?"

Even the therapists were in tears. But there was more. Much more.

"When I lost the baby, it seemed that my life was over. Not just as a mother but as a person. How can any mother, and I was a mother once, don't forget, even bear to think that that her baby would die inside her? I failed my baby, Pat. I let it die. Why should I have deserved to have a normal life. Why, Pat, why? Dad gave us bad genes. It was just a matter of time before I would get it. Being an alcoholic. It was a curse on us."

It was the one and only time that she looked at Pat through the whole of their six weeks of therapy.

"But I was given another chance. You don't often get another chance in life. I let Dr Hither down. Let him down badly and then he wasn't there for me. He wasn't there to catch me. To catch when I fell, into that, that, life you all thought was my own making.

"You may all think I'm selfish but I'm not. I wasn't selfish. I was never selfish, or at least I didn't mean to be. I was alone, confused, frightened – all those things, when Jim died. Then I fell, not just physically but slipped and fell into that well, that pit that swallowed me whole. Every so often, I would come up for air with a glimmer of hope. Drink turns you into a monster. You're always in denial, always in two minds about drinking, but the drink always wins and that makes you feel guilty, so

guilty. You know, it's just so strange that letting someone in to fix my tap would mean me sitting here, a recovering alcoholic with some hope for a better life. A life without Dad, without Mum, without Jim, without Babs. All I've got now is you, Pat, and I promise I won't hurt you again."

Pat could barely move. Transfixed. Rooted to the spot. She put down the bag that she always kept on her lap like Linus' blanket so that she could beat a hasty retreat when sessions were over. But this time, she simply placed it on the chair and walked over to where Peggy was sitting.

Peggy got up too quickly and toppled over, but Pat was ready to catch her and broke her fall, also tumbling over in the process. The silence was interrupted by shrill cachinnation that grew louder by the second. There were tears. Of laughter. Of joy. Of relief and of hope.

"You silly old trout, Peggy luv. 'Ow could I desert you, my big sis. Do'ya remember that time when that farmer chased you down the field when we used to go 'opping. You jumped over that fence like a jack rabbit and went flying. You only went and landed on me. We was covered in mud, we was. Mum wasn't best pleased."

They salvaged their dignity and helped each other up.

A month later, Peggy, Pat and Rene were dressed up the nines as they went out for a curry at the Elephant. It seemed like only yesterday, but yesterday was never to be. Only tomorrow.

Chapter 15

Place of Rest

Friday, 3 February 2006
Bluemere Multi-Disciplinary Meeting
Present
Dr Raz Hughes, Consultant Old Age Psychiatrist
Caesar Abimbola, Deputy Unit Manager
Sara Meadway-Hull, Occupational Therapist
John Minktileau Physiotherapist

Peggy Lighterman (d.o.b. 7 March 1933)
Diagnosis: Alcohol Related Dementia ICD F10.73

Peggy has been on the unit now for 9 months. She has become progressively more frail and needs the assistance of 2 people with walking. She is both verbally aggressive and now sexually disinhibited with male staff, who try and maintain her dignity when this happens. She appears in pain when she mobilises, mainly in her right hip, which shows evidence of osteoarthritis. Peggy has been prescribed soluble paracetamol but not strong opioids, owing the side-effects of constipation and over-sedation. As she spends more time in bed during the day, she is at risk of pressure sores and had a hospital bed and ripple mattress to minimise this risk. Self-care remains challenging and staff now wear personal protective equipment (face masks) when delivering personal care, as she spits at them. She also continues to bite, scratch and hit staff. Last week, there was an incident recorded when she kicked a staff member so hard in the shin, they have gone off sick. Peggy continues to be visited by her IMCA, Jayne Leggitt but does not have any other visitors. Relatives and friends are very understanding of her behaviour and staff seem to think that she recognises one of the visitors from when she was younger, which is possible. However, there have been occasions when some visitors have become upset when she has become angry with staff and threatens to "burn the place down".

Peggy takes a long time to eat and sometimes eats food with her hands, therefore requiring supervision during mealtimes. Medication is given covertly in food such as yoghurt, jam or hot chocolate. This includes newly introduced medication for dementia. Sleep remains poor and she remains restless, not settling until about 3am, when she falls asleep in the day room. The unit has purchased a special riser recliner chair for her, to minimise the upheaval of moving her back to her room in such circumstances. Peggy requires full personal care and is incontinent of urine and faeces.

Concealed in that frail body and fragile mind were three things that sparked glimpses of the old Peggy. First there was custard, then orange squash and then music. Custard was always going to be a family favourite, with Pearce Duff just around the corner as she was growing up. Squash was also part of Peggy's food and drink Top of the Pops, especially her penchant for bourbons and custard creams. As for music, Dr Hither could have told you that he'd seen music bring back that glint in the eyes of people with dementia. It sparks a deep emotional connection with the past.

When she first arrived on the unit, Peggy used to strut her stuff to *Rock Around the Clock* and sing her lungs out at the top of her voice to Is *This the Way to Amarillo?*

Friday, 7 July 2006

Bluemere Unit Nursing Entry 11:00

Peggy has been spending more time in bed and is looking drowsy. She also seems chesty. Observations: Temp 38.0. Pulse 90 and regular, BP 130/80. Oxygen Sats 91%

The GP has been called.

"Peggy luv. Just look at you. Ice cream all over that frock. What a messy little madam you are. That's the last time I let you buy your own 99." Ice cream melts like ice cream always does, but with children, it just gets that bit messier when they let it trickle onto their tops and when they get it on their hands, it soon gets wiped onto some part of their apparel. Usually on a newly washed piece of clothing. Pat and Babs giggled.

"Peggy is a messy madam. Peggy is a messy madam."

Peggy groaned and coughed. That raspy cough that never stops until you take another deep breath. She turned onto her left side to get more comfortable.

"Look what I got you girls from one of my mates down the docks. 'Is wife works down Shuttleworths. She got a couple of boxes for 'im and he owed me a favour, so 'ere you are." He gave that cheeky wink that only Cyril could give and sat them all on his knee as they stuffed their mouths, enticed by the sweet, creamy taste of chocolate heaven. A voice reverberated from the kitchen. "Don't you let them 'ave too much, Cyril, else they'll be sick."

Peggy's breath quickened, her cough now hacking. The doctor called to say that he was on his way.

"This special award goes to Peggy Lighterman. Peggy was very brave yesterday and this special badge is to reward that bravery." It was two weeks after the bombing raid and the school had re-opened. Rapturous applause and the occasional wolf whistle echoed across the school assembly hall as Peggy held aloft the symbol of her gallantry. She would treasure it for the rest of her life.

The doctor arrived and opened his bag, He rubbed the stethoscope bell against his hand to warm it up. Two nurses helped sat Peggy up. Her torpor had drained her of all energy.

"Yes, I can hear some crackles and wheezes and you mentioned that she's coughing up yellow phlegm. We'd better get her started on antibiotics and please make sure that she's drinking a least a litre of fluid per day." The nurses gave Peggy her first dose of antibiotic within an hour. "I would normally have sent Peggy to hospital, but we have an advance directive made after she was in hospital three years ago which states that she wanted to be treated wherever she was living and not admitted to hospital." Peggy remained in a deep slumber.

"Pegs. Promise me something. Promise me that you'll light a candle for me on my birthday." Jim was slipping away. Peggy squeezed his hand tightly. "Yes, luv. Even in my dying breath, you will be in my heart."

She was now drifting in and out of consciousness, her breathing shallow and laboured.

"Mummy, Mummy. Come and see what I've drawn, Mummy!" David looked just like his father, Jim. His long curly black hair and long eyelashes were adorable. Peggy had longed to see her son and knew that, one day, they would be re-united. "Come on then, little man. Show Mummy what you've drawn." David tugged at Peggy's dress and led her to his bedroom. The Elephant looked different from his bedroom. There was even a new market – The Room in the Elephant – teeming with people. Peggy glanced back and saw a picture on the floor, drawn in red felt tip. It was a little boy holding hands with his mother. "Do you like it, Mummy? I want to be good, Mummy. I want to be like you."

Peggy gasped for breath. A nurse came running. There was no one to call. No friend, no son or daughter, no distant cousin.

"Peggy. What a pleasant surprise. I heard about what happened. I just came to pay my respects. It's a real shame that I couldn't be there. A real shame." He shook his head and closed the door one last time. He had said his final goodbye to Peggy and to Bermondsey but would cherish his memories. Every single last one of them.

If he had still been there when Peggy was in need, he would have done the same as Dave had done. Treat patients as people first then as patients, he would say. Don't launch into asking if they hear voices or drink too much. Take time to get to know them. It could be as simple as asking them about a picture and where it was taken. Where they got those ornaments. How they spend their day. That's the human connection that sows the seeds of trust and hope. Without it, change cannot happen. It remains no more than two disconnected objects moving in silos, just drifting in the vain hope that, in time, all will be well.

As Peggy drifted away to dance with the angels, tears streamed down her face. She was finally re-united with her family. Dad, Jim and now David. She's said goodbye to Dr Hither and would meet Mum soon, no doubt.

These were not the tears of stigma. Of sorrow or shame. Of desolation or despair. These were the tears of the hidden and forgotten. Of the invisible addict. These were the tears of thunder that had ripped her world apart. No one caught her when she fell. Again, and again, and again. Help came. But it was too late.

Peggy opened her eyes and smiled to the world. And in an instant, she was gone.

Epilogue

As Rene laid the wreath at Peggy's graveside, she felt a pang of guilt. She would treasure those memories and knew that Peggy had become gripped by the bottle. Her dear friend was not the first to have fallen foul of it and wouldn't be the last. But she couldn't help feeling that there was surely something that could have been done to rescue Peggy from the burning deck of alcoholism. Bermondsey had resisted change but then so had Peggy. But what if help had come sooner?

If she had cancer or something other physical malady, there would have been help at hand. People would have bent over backwards to help her. Done everything in their power to just keep trying. So where was everyone when she needed them most? If only someone had only tried to engage her better, just kept persisting, always looking for a new solution. Perhaps they could have tried to help her with practical things instead of going in with all guns blazing. Maybe then she could have warmed to this approach. In time, she might have finally come clean about her drinking without fear of rebuke. It would have needed patience and determination, but she would have got there. Resistance, denial and ambivalence are the hallmarks of alcoholism. They can't just be fixed by a stern talking to or a tablet to suddenly make things better.

Finding ways to encourage people to change requires skill, perseverance and some ingenuity.

If Peggy had been given the opportunity to recover at her own pace, she would have surely stood a better chance of recovery. Instead, she was left to languish and fester in a musty, dusty, dingy space that was once her beautiful home. She was left with a life with no dignity or quality. For Rene, there were too many *what ifs*. What if Jim and Babs hadn't died? What if Rene had done more for her? What if Peggy hadn't lost a child? Would she still be with us? We will never know but we do know that Peggy's life could have been turned around. Instead, the petty boundaries set by those whose job it is to serve and protect the sick and vulnerable had failed her. We had failed her. Society had failed her.

As the untimely death of Peggy Lighterman passes us by, we know that that there will continue to be many more Peggys. Many more people lost in the mists of time, never to be heard of again. Time and time and time again, our blind spot becomes larger. Surely not an older woman drinking. That too, a retired teacher. A fine upstanding pillar of society. They couldn't possibly succumb to such a moral weakness. Surely not? There were always opportunities to help Peggy. All were now wasted but we have been offered a taste of what could have been for our lovely Peggy. The Dr Hithers of this world remain few and far between, but they are always out there. But they need to shout with once voice, banging the drum of reason. No one is born an alcoholic.

But to judge it with the stigma and prejudice that has surrounded it for time immemorial does us all a disservice. It could happen to any of us. Our sister or brother, son or daughter, mother or father, grandparents or grandchildren.

Even our doctor, nurse, priest or teacher. The day that a broken leg and broken heart are to be judged as equally deserving of treatment will be the day that humankind becomes truly enlightened.

Each generation leaves, in some form or other, an indelible imprint on the hearts and souls of the next. Some will have left a legacy of noble pursuits and endeavours that have changed the world, others have breezed through with an Epicurean hedonism that leaves them as no more than passengers adrift a passing sigh in the deep exhalation of mankind.

Peggy had not a bad bone in her body, but we are left screaming into the face of a deterministic rhetoric that we will never fully understand. Why some remain on the wrong side of fate will never be fully known. We can only be eternally thankful for the favourable hand that is dealt to us and we should all be grateful, as we count our blessings, that there but for the grace of God go I.

THE END